"Live in such a way that even if given another opportunity to live your life all over again, you would still choose to live it exactly the same way that you are living your life now."

William B. Girao, *Enjoy Life: The Message of Ecclesiastes*

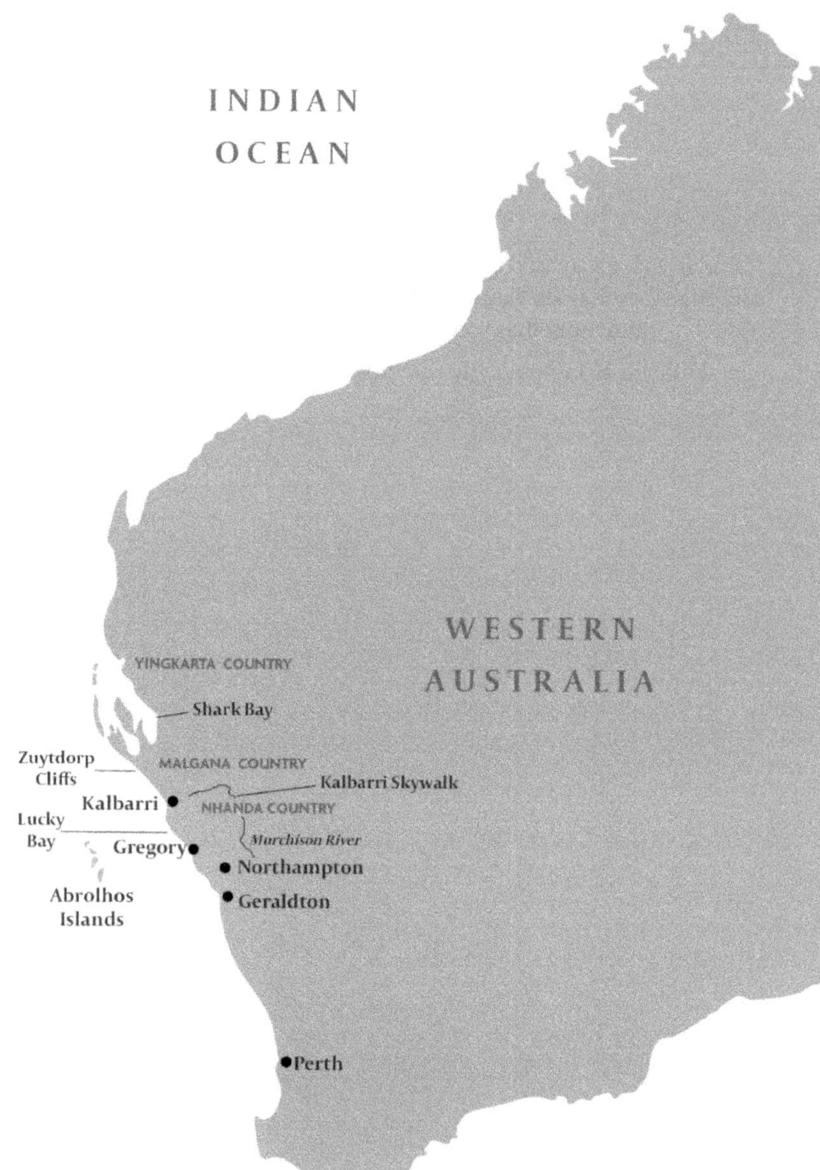
INDIAN
OCEAN
WESTERN
AUSTRALIA
YINGKARTA COUNTRY
Shark Bay
Zuytdorp
Cliffs
MALGANA COUNTRY
Kalbarri Skywalk
Kalbarri
NHANDA COUNTRY
Lucky
Bay
Murchison River
Gregory
Northampton
Abrolhos
Islands
Geraldton
Perth

PROLOGUE

Kalbarri Skywalk – iStock Photos

January 2025, in the Lyons Den, Lucky Bay, Kalbarri in the mid-west of Western Australia

"EVERYONE HAS A STORY to tell as their life rolls on," says my best friend, Willie Mack. "You can't deny it."

He's the smart one. He's Scottish. Been in Australia for six years and still talking like he's just arrived. "Never mind my accent," he tells me. "Australia's rubbed off on me in other ways."

It has too.

It's like he's one of us.

That's why I consider him my twin. My bruh.

My twin? You wouldn't think so.

We couldn't look more different. Me with my brown skin and black hair, him with his ginger hair and those orange freckles all over him, the blotchy kind that don't leave much room for the skin. He's stockier than me at five six, with an interesting face. Green eyes with a dreamy look to them until he fires up with a joke or a pun or he's taking the piss, then they light up like you wouldn't believe and it cracks you up to look at him with his lopsided grin and a single dimple sliced into his left cheek. A snub nose and ginger eyebrows complete the picture. Put him in a kilt with a set of bagpipes and he'd look the part as a backup piper in AC/DC for Bon Scott singing *It's a Long Way to the Top*.

We started off calling him Bluey at first, but he preferred Willie Mack. More class, he said, and it stuck.

He's fifteen, like me. We both just turned—me on 1 January, 2025, him on the eleventh, exactly a week ago.

So we're both Alpha gen, along with the other two billion Alphas. Already the greatest number of the same generation on earth ever.

Alpha says it all, I reckon.

We're two Alpha males, sitting at the Hexagonal Table right now, in the Lyons Den, our shack, hidden among the dunes at Lucky Bay.

"You're in God's own country," my dad's always telling us. "And don't you two forget it".

Except Willie Mack's an atheist, or so he informed me last year.

"Why an atheist?" I asked him at the time.

"God knows," he replied with a tilt of his head and a lift of his right eyebrow. "He's kept us guessing once too often, maybe. He starts off turning on the lights, then keeps us in the dark ever since."

Me? I'm not too sure. Maybe it pays to be wary.

So anyway, back to our conversation.

"If we've all got a story to tell about our lives, is it fact or fiction?" I ask him.

"Fact, unless you're lying to yourself. I figure it's because we live in a world where things are happening all the time. Nothing endures. We're changing every moment. You, me and all the other nine billion people crowding this little blue dot of a planet–which is definitely flat, by the way."

"Flat?"

"Yep. All the way round."

When I snort out a laugh, "If you don't believe me, start walking it," he says. "If you keep going it'll be flat all the way, until you get back to where you started from."

I recognise his way of foxing with words with a weird logic to them, so I take a deep breath and know it's seaweed season. Great piles of it washed up in a brown knee-deep row at the high-tide mark along the beach, the fresh salty stink of it reaching us. It's full of sand midgies that bite. We've both got itchy lumps on our calves from last night's fishing. The lamplight attracted them until we switched it off. We caught some juvenile and jumbo Tailor and a decent sized Bluebone. The Tailor we threw back to live on after the adrenalin rush of the fight, and we enjoyed a monster fried fillet of the best fish in the world each for dinner, with more in the fridge for tonight. With the skin on. Charred and crispy on the barbecue. No blue bones—I used the pliers. Yum.

"Everyone has a part to play in their story." Willie Mack goes on. "Everyone has a role. No one misses out on aiming for a goal. Doesn't matter how insignificant or important. From choofing on a vape to running a marathon, say, or a gazillion other things."

"What about someone with a lousy memory? Someone with brain damage who's forgotten who they are?"

"Them too, the poor buggers, because nothing happens to them all the time, even though they may not know it. We act out our roles from one second to the next according to what happened the moment before, to keep our story going as the plot thickens. And it's the roles we remember playing that tell us who we are. Our selves. We could be four plus four heroes. Could be enemies or antagonists. Or one of the chat, one of the spectators."

"Okay, I hear you. But what if there's a change of scene? Like, I'm one person at school and someone else at home?"

"Sure, when the circumstances change, so does the story,

but it's still an ongoing narrative. Just a human being doing something different. But you know you've changed because you're doing things differently. The voice in your head reminds you."

"The voice? You hear voices?"

"It's a metaphor, bruh. Not a voice as such, but a voice*over*. A storyteller spinning your yarns as things happen so you can make sense of yourself. Not a fixed self. Not a sky-pilot sitting inside your skull, some ghostly permanent you telling you what to do or how to feel."

"You're losing me, Willie Mack. Now I don't have a self? I'm getting confused."

"No dramas, Summer. So am I. That's our storytellers spinning the yarn of the two of us right here, right now, in the Lyons Den, wondering what the hell I'm yapping on about, who the hell we are and what the hell life is all about."

"So, what comes next?"

"Who bloody knows? Johnny Elliott?"

I can't stop laughing.

Bloody nose. Johnny Elliott.

Almost fall off my chair.

Almost wet my pants.

But a second later I get to thinking about what he said regarding our stories, and I remember the day they found the sixth Alpha Bruh of the Hexagonal Table, dead, on the rocks beside the Murchison River, 100 metres below the Kalbarri Skywalk. The shock and rush of grief tear me apart, and it's like I'm being stabbed in the chest again and again.

That was a fortnight ago, on 4 January, in between our birthdays.

Naked, they said.

Naked? No way. Not Moses Buzzacott. Not our "Mozzie". The youngest of us, because his birthday is on the 28 December, twelve months after me and Willie Mack. He's always the last to come swimming in the nick because his *kuca*, his nuts, have only just descended and he hasn't grown many of his pubic feathers yet.

It's not his fault, but add to that his Christian name, Moses—his dead Italian mother was a Catholic and all her nine kids have biblical names—and he's vulnerable to bullying.

In spite of that, or maybe because of it, he has to be the best boxer I've ever seen. Orthodox, brave, flash-quick and elusive, we never saw him lose a fight, often against kids way bigger than him.

We miss him something terrible—and now we're five.

Was he pushed? Or did he jump?

Either way, we must find out the truth, to get the stories of our lives straight.

Chapter 1

Apache Chief Geronimo, taken by Warren Mack Oliver, 1907

January 2025, in Geraldton, in the mid-west of Western Australia

CALL ME SUMA.

That's Suma, pronounced "Sooma", but some years ago—never mind how long precisely—someone gave me the nickname "Summer".

The first time they came up with it I was wild. A girl's name. I hated it, but I was a shy and quiet kid then, new to Geraldton, and couldn't do anything about it. I gritted my teeth and bore it.

So it stuck.

Things are different now. I'm not the skinny little runt they pushed around in Primary school. No sir. I'm fifteen-years-old, and built, with so many hairs sprouting under both my armpits I've lost count. Not to mention my legs and other places.

"Summer?" I said the other day when Johnny Elliott called me that. "*Summer?* That's a girl's name. You call me Summer one more time and you'll have me to deal with."

"Hey, Summer," Johnny Elliott laughed, then added in a high-pitched zesty voice, "must be because you're so *hot*, girl."

Having little or no hesitation in my mind, and nothing in particular to hold me back, I clocked him one, broke his nose and had him visiting the watery part of the world when he burst into tears.

That put things nicely in perspective.

But the next day I got to thinking about it.

Summer. Hot. Hot as hell.

Hellish hot, in fact. Especially here in Geraldton, in the mid-west of Western Australia where we're from.

It suddenly sounded manly to me.

Manly, like the whaler Queequeg in *Moby Dick*, the harpooner with the tatts and brown skin, like mine. We're studying him this year at school, in old man "Twiga" Gammie's English class. He's a cranky, sarcastic old teacher we secretly have a lot of time and respect for, because he's old school and keeps us under his thumb. In his classes you can hear a pin drop. He walks with crutches strapped to his arms because he was paralysed from the hips down with polio when he was a kid. He looks like a giraffe when you watch him walk side-on, with his long forelegs leaving his back legs behind. That's why we christened him "Twiga". He migrated here from Kenya in the 1960's and twiga's the Swahili word for giraffe. He joined the school two years ago.

My school? That's the George Grey College in Geraldton.

And not only Queequeg—Suma also refers to the Apache Indians in Mexico and the USA. That's why my dad chose it. Think of Geronimo. Or Cochise and Sitting Bull. Even Victorio. All great names and courageous leaders. I like to think I'm following in their footsteps, even if I have a fair way to go. At least I have their roadmap.

So I've recently come to like the name Summer and no longer mind, long as everyone acknowledges I'm a bloke. Even if they don't, well, that's okay too. Because *I* know for sure.

So does Charlotte Marks. Green-eyed, strawberry-blond Charlie M with her fringe, the Nhanda-Irish sis with freckles across her nose who's turned fourteen. I've seen the way you look at me. Stirs me up. I'm not gunna lie, I reckon we're thirsty for each other. One of these days I'll get round to talking to you.

Oh, I forgot to mention—my full name's Suma Dartson.

Dartson. Weird, hey? Bet you haven't heard it before.

I googled it and found it's the 4,649,889th most common surname in the world. According to Wikipedia they all live in the USA. Yanks. They claim to be the best at everything so they've even stolen my surname. Bugger that. How come Google didn't know about us Dartsons up around Shark Bay? Forty-five of us at the last count, when we got together at Grandma Milly's funeral service in Denham three months ago. Eighty, actually, when you add our close relatives, the Curries, in with us. Five Malgana Yamaji families descended from four brothers and a sister still living. The wise ones we all respect. Don't step out of line, my cousin brothers and sisters. That's us—the Dartsons and the Curries. We're all related.

It was Willie Mac—the brightest one in English Lit among us bruhs by far—who pointed out some time back my name spelled "Nostradamus" back to front.

"You know Nostradamus?" he asked.

"No, I don't."

"He was a Frenchman who predicted the future four hundred years ago. Hitler and the destruction of Germany. The assassination of the Kennedy brothers. The twin towers. Trump and his yellow toupée making a comeback. Even the apocalypse and the end of us all."

"Sounds interesting. I'll google him."

"He might surprise you."

"Could be he had second sight, like some of my Malgana mob. Always reading each other's minds."

"You too?"

"Sometimes. Mum says I've had the gift since I was a little kid."

"You're telepathic?"

"So she says."

Then he grinned. "I knew it."

"You knew it?"

"Yep. Something told me you would be."

The coming apocalypse and the end of us all? I thought. *Now that's a worry, when you think about it.*

And we do, us Alpha Bruhs of the Hexagonal Table.

We think about it.

Often.

Because it's an elephant.

An elephant, you ask?

Yep. Cat-, dog- and elephant-, they're our three degrees of catastrophe in rising order. If one of us is in the shit and needs help, he can tell the rest of us how urgent it is with a single word. "It's a cat-," and we take our time. "It's a dog-" and we get there soon as we can. "It's an elephant-" and we're up and sprinting out the door to help.

We have a code of conduct too, would you believe? And a national anthem.

You want the code? *The only rule you never break is the rule that says you can break every rule in the book if it helps you reach your goals. Loyalty. Honesty. Wisdom.*

That might sound like a load of crap to you, but think about it. You've only got to look around. We don't want to get to twenty-nine and feel so lonely, disconnected and purposeless that our lives and everything we've ever done seem meaningless. When we've lost our culture and our self-respect. When we don't know who we are and wonder what the hell being a man really means as we sink another Bourbon neat, or drag on a cone before sucking up a line through a rolled up ten, if we've got one. Or, worse still, attach the rope to a beam or the hose to the exhaust pipe with the engine running.

We're Alpha gens and we're starting our journey to manhood young is all.

Our national anthem is Prince's song *1999*. That was Willie Mack's idea, too. He thought of it after finding out that Prince wrote the lyrics after seeing a documentary about Nostradamus prophesying the end of the universe as we know it.

If we're all gunna die, let's have a great time going.

We sing a mixture of the verses whenever we feel like it. It's a bonding thing. Especially when we're accompanying the blaring Bluetooth stereo in bruh "Tiny" Jameson's Jeep Wrangler when he's driving us up to Lucky Bay in the early dawn on the weekend with the roof off.

With the wind blasting through your hair and singing your guts out at a hundred k's an hour, we're already partying, like it's 1999, no questions asked. That's when you know you're *alive*, and you're sharing the thrill of it with your five mates.

There's nothing like it.

No sir!

Chapter 2

As for my telepathic gift, well, I have these strange dreams—you could call them nightmares—and when I tell Mum about them, it turns out they predict the *past*, not the future.

Maybe that's because my name spells Nostradamus back to front. I get things *manda* about. *Manda*—that's Malgana for backside—so arse about, if you prefer it in Australian. Forgive me if I use the occasional Malgana word while telling you my story. I've already used *kuca*, as you know. I'm a proud Malgana Yamaji boy and I'm picking up the vocab and need the practice. Trust me, I'll always translate it for you

So, dreams.

It sounds strange, but it's true.

I have these dreams and when Mum or Dad interprets them, they're about something that's already happened that I didn't know about.

You want an example?

Here's a simple one.

Short and sweet.

Last November, I'm being chased by these faceless zombies like I'm in a horror movie straight out of Netflix. Half a dozen of them, armed with pointed sticks. And I mean really pointed, sharpened and charred black in the bushfire raging round us. They're trying to poke my eyeballs out so I can no longer see. To lose my second sight. I run like hell through the flames and wake up screaming, my heart rattling in my chest at a million beats a minute and sweating like a pig—which they do, by the way, just less than us.

When I tell Dad about it, he surprises me. He's talkative for once. That's unusual for him. He usually gives me the silent treatment.

"Oh, that's easy, Sonny," he says. He calls me Sonny, preferring it to Suma, even though he chose the name. "That's got to be Olly Brierley up on Tamala Station the other day. Fire went through the paddocks a month ago and he was fixing up the fencing to keep the feral goats and emus out. When he tautened the barbed wire in one section, he overdid the tension and it snapped. Sprang back and caught him in his right eye. He's still in Carnarvon Hospital last I heard. He'll never see through it again. He'll probably wear an eyepatch like Sammy Davis Junior next time we see him in the Waterfront Hotel, and we'll never hear the end of it."

Here's a better one. I clearly remember it because it recurred several times in November 2020, when I was ten.

It gave me what my Great Grandad Wally called the "screaming meemies" when he was still alive. Or so my dad told me when he used the phrase once.

"Don't *do* that, Meg," he shouted at my four-year-old sister when she picked her nose and was considering eating it. "You're giving me the screaming meemies!"

I warned her later when we were alone that if she kept doing it she'd pull her brains out one day, and that got her attention.

Anyway.

"The screaming meemies?" I asked him. "I haven't heard that one before"

"You know your Great Grandad Wally was in the trenches at Amiens for a time during World War I? Well, he ducked for cover when those German artillery shells came screaming overhead. *Meeeemie.* That's the sound they made. Thankfully none of them had his name on it."

Anyway, forget about the screaming meemies if it bothers you.

Let's put it this way.

I'm scared shitless. Which means the opposite, when you come to think about it. Check your underpants next time if you don't believe me.

Because my dream is about snakes.

The really poisonous kind.

With fangs like hypodermics, dripping yellow venom if you get too close.

I know it's yellow because I dream in colour.

Full blown, like colour's my thing.

And in the dreams that really matter I'm not running for my life from zombies with pointed sticks, or getting lost and panicked in some unknown city, or flying across some green landscape I've never seen before, avoiding the power lines when I come in to land.

No.

I'm *there*.

I'm taking part.

Sometimes I have an active speaking part. Other times I'm an observer. Sometimes both. I never know which it's gunna be until the reel starts running.

In this dream I'm on some tropical island in the Atlantic centuries ago. Not sure where it is or when. Off Africa, I guess, because the natives are black, except for one who's mixed blood and brown, like me.

It starts off I'm in the local hospital, carrying the leather bag for some bloke I vaguely already know. From some other dream, maybe? Another life? I'm not sure.

Turns out he's the surgeon aboard a three masted sailing ship he points out, anchored in the bay. So I hold his bag open as the local pharmacist fills it with the medical supplies the surgeon needs. Weird stuff. Some I remember because Mum has them in her pantry. Cinnamon and caraway seeds for heartburn and indigestion. A handful of shrivelled roots of Ipecac to make you vomit if you've overdosed. A sack of dried cinchona bark you crush up and make a drink for malaria.

And then the pharmacist alarms me.

He reaches into the back of his cabinet and takes out two corked test tubes containing small amounts of a pale-yellow liquid.

"Would you have any use for one of these? It's Gabon viper venom," he says.

I watch the surgeon holding it up to the light. "Interesting. What do you use it for?"

"We add it to strengthen some potions we use for leprosy and smallpox. This is spare."

The surgeon shakes his head "I don't think we'll need it."

Before the pharmacist can replace them in the cabinet, I reach across and snatch one. I turn it this way and that, then give it a good shake.

The liquid moves like golden mercury.

"Where do you get it from?" I ask.

"We have a snake pit here. The Angolares who looks after it is a sorcerer. He's been bitten so many times he's immune." He looks me up and down, from my bare feet to the top of my head. "I can show you if you like," he says, as I hand him back the tube.

So we walk through the town. I remember shady mango trees packed with orange ripening fruit and dark green maize and sugar cane plantations beneath the palm trees rising up the mountain slopes that disappear into rain clouds to our right. The simple, single storey houses with one front door, a step, and a window either side, all painted in different pastel colours, like a kid's drawing.

Different pastel colours. I like that.

And a French flag hanging on a pole. Red, white and blue if there was a wind, but there's not. It's too early in the day.

When we reach the snake pit, the snake whisperer is already hard at it. He isn't wearing shoes. His bare feet are sticking out from cowhide protectors stretching from his ankle to his knee.

He's standing among the snakes in a circular pit, twenty metres across and a metre deep.

It's full of writhing and sleeping snakes of different types.

There must be a hundred of them.

I don't recognise any. No Dugites. No King Browns or Gwardar. No Death Adders. But the pharmacist has mentioned the Gabon viper.

That must be the snake he has coiled around his forearm.

It's the length of my arm, the ribs of its thick body shifting and gliding beneath the glistening skin as if it's trying to free itself from the Angolare's grip behind its head. The scales on its back are patterned in brown and purple pentagons, while the belly is pale gold. It has two blue-green horns on its broad skull and a bony ridge across its gleaming eyes.

It looks both beautiful and evil.

Like it's thinking *Come closer, human. I can't wait to sink my fangs into you.*

The Angolares holds the monster's mouth open against the lip of a test tube while he teases out the fangs. I'm shocked by their curving length and thinness—if I told you three centimetres you wouldn't believe me, but I wouldn't be exaggerating. They're encased in a silky white skin webbing he pushes back into its jaw with a bronze rod; and as he massages its head with his thumb the yellow venom squirts down the glass.

Then he corks it.

Watching, I feel as if I'm being hypnotised, marvelling at the slow-motion care with which he holds the tube and works the rod with the fingers of his left hand, as if he's practised using chopsticks.

He gently places the snake back on the dirt floor, stroking it before wandering across to us almost carelessly to give the pharmacist the tube.

Before I can stop him, he reaches up and without a word he grabs me by the armpits. He lifts me high into the pit, stretching out so that I have a metre or two to walk back to the wall,

Then he climbs out himself and watches my reaction with the others.

I stand paralysed.

I have never felt so terrified.

Then a rush of adrenalin burns through my chest and I'm on the verge of passing out as I take one faltering step forward and feel the cold body of a viper crack beneath the sole of my right foot. I look down as the snake rears back like a powerful spring and strikes at my calf, its mouth gaping.

I wake screaming before the bite and Mum rushes in to see what's woken me.

I'm sweating again and shaking like a penguin in a blizzard as she hugs me.

Like I said, I was ten years old.

We told Dad a fortnight later, when he returned from Denham after a Snapper fishing trip. We were at breakfast. He was making toast. He listened, thought about it for a moment and then slowly nodded without a comment, as was his way.

It didn't pay to push him.

Then he said at last, "That can only mean two things, Sonny. You're walking in the footsteps of Geronimo, so you have to watch your step. You have to be careful. Be precise and aware. On the ball. All the time. Those Diamond Rattlesnakes in your path are out to do you harm before you become a teenager and then a man."

He turned back to the toaster to retrieve his slices, then sat and spread the honey. Concentrating, by the looks. Grim and silent as usual. Not glancing up, before he took a bite. And then another. And a third.

"That's only one," I dared to break the silence at last, the only sound the crunching as he chewed his toast. "What's the other?"

"The other what?"

"You said my dream has two meanings."

"Oh, right. Yes. That. Well. Your Uncle "Storky" Heron out on Murchison House Station the other night. He took his torch and went up to the freezer in the shearing shed to get a leg of lamb. When he lifted the lid, he felt something hit his ankle as he reached in. Didn't think too much about it till he got to the door and looked down. There was this two metre Dugite with its fangs caught in his West Coast Eagles footy socks. It was angry as, according to him."

"That's it?"

"That's it. Just as well he had his socks rolled down and thick right where it bit, he reckons."

He took another bite, and I could see his mind wandering off. Back to Shark Bay and pulling in another Snapper trap, most probably.

"So, what did he do?"

He looked up sharply as he swallowed. "What do you think he did? He hit it with the leg of lamb, you drongo. Just as well it was frozen."

And that was that.

I'd predicted the past, and the past event had happened a week ago. My prophetic dreams were pointless.

Drongo.

That's me.

I'm the middle kid, with my younger sister Meg still at home. She's four and picks her nose, as I've mentioned. It's my older brother Billy, five years older than me, whose shit doesn't stink according to Dad. Straight A's and studying Law at the WA Uni. Me, I'm a C grade student and I'm okay with that. If I earn a B it's the occasional miracle. Except for art. Art's an A most of the time.

"Art?" Dad said once, checking my report. "What's the point, Sonny? What are we wasting good money on you for? You'll end up painting boomerangs for the tourists or designing patterns for the materials used in some flea-bitten dressmaker's shop at best. Art's for dreamers in my book."

Dreamers.

Exactly!

So I almost made a decision not to tell anyone about them in future.

Until my Uncle, Lennard Currie, the one outstanding success in our family with glass sculptures he has created all over the world—including the famous glass cenotaph in Fremantle dedicated to the twenty thousand blackfellas who died on our behalf during the invasion—told me to keep a diary and show him, when he visited us a few days after I had the snake dream.

He's one of our Malgana Yamaji men of High Degree. He's over seventy years old now. With a full mop of white hair and eyebrows to match, he has these startling eyes. One's a brilliant blue, the other brown. I've known him all my life so I don't notice them, but I can imagine if you met him for the first time you'd get a shock. He thinks it's a throwback, proving he's related to a blue-eyed Dutch sailor who survived a shipwreck three centuries ago in the north-west. He's six foot three and still straight as a piece of four by two, provided you don't notice his developing pot.

You don't mess with him and he'll treat you the way you want to be treated as a kid—with mutual respect, without being patronised.

Step out of line though, different story.

His partner, Aunty Alicia, is a Mexican twenty years younger than him. She's a linguist working at the Yamaji Language Centre keeping all our languages alive. I visit her at the Centre sometimes when she's up from Perth, but that isn't often these days. She's part Tarahumaran Indian and she's the one told Dad about the Suma Apaches. Her tribe used to be at war with them centuries ago in the mountains in north-west Mexico, she says.

So I suppose I owe her my name.

Thanks Aunty Alicia.

"Your dreams could have a deeper meaning, Suma," Uncle Lennard said. "Could be the ancestors communicating with you. I don't just think it's possible. I'm sure of it." He placed a hand on my shoulder and squeezed. I can still feel it to this day if I try hard enough and it's comforting. "That three-masted ship out in the bay. You never know, it could be survivors of the *Zuytdorp* wreck communicating with you, and you could be another Carl Jung, dreaming of blood all over Germany and the Western Front a year before the First World War."

I wondered about the way he looked at me that day, like he knew something about me I didn't and was keeping it to himself, but I took him at his word.

And Carl Jung dreaming of blood? I haven't got round to googling him yet. You can give Google a go too, if you're not sure.

Uncle Lennard has researched the shipwreck of the *Zuytdorp* on the cliffs north of Kalbarri, after all. He's even written a novel about it, but couldn't get it published in the 1990's. He says thirty rejection slips was all it took for him to stick it in a bottom drawer, and it hasn't seen the light of day since then. I must get him to let me read it when I'm older if he doesn't mind.

"Take my advice," he told me that day. "Record your dreams for me, and read *Carpet Of Silver* if there's a copy in the school library. It came out in 1996, the same year I got the 30th rejection slip for my novel. That'll give you a good idea what I'm talking about. It'll give you all the facts about the

Zuytdorp shipwreck and it's an easy read." Then he chuckled. "Easier than mine, by all accounts."

Before he turned away he asked me, "Have you got a mobile phone, Suma?"

"Yes, I do. An Apple iPhone 12. Mum bought me one last month when they came out, so we could keep in touch when I'm at school in the boarding house."

"So have I. Feel free to call me and we can talk about your latest dream at any time, if you want to get it off your chest."

We swapped numbers and I felt privileged.

So while I still told Mum about my dreams, I've also recorded them ever since. I'm about to fill my second exercise book and I'll get round to showing them to Uncle Lennard when I'm good and ready.

One of these fine days.

He knows about them anyway, because we've spoken on the phone.

With him I'm certain it wouldn't have been in one ear and out the other, like Dad.

Chapter 3

January 2025, at the Lyons Den, Lucky Bay.

OUR SHACK, THE LYONS Den, is a sturdy corrugated iron two-room lean-to standing at the western end of old man Ben Lyons's property. It's in the dunes, two hundred metres from the ocean. It's protected from the winds and most days and nights we can hear the crashing of the waves on the rocks around the lagoon and smell the salt.

There's a twelve-foot tinny on a trailer by the door, with a 25 horse Johnson on the back.

It's magic, as long as you can stand the heat. Especially in midsummer, when it can get hot as a firey's nut sack on Black Saturday—google it if you don't know. The worst ever, in 2009, and 173 Victorians dead.

No worries for us with the heat, though. We have the sea to cool off in, and we can dive on the outer reef to catch a bunch of crays for dinner.

Crays? You ask. Or Rock Lobster?

Who cares? It's always been crays for us, unless you want to be politically correct—but that's not us.

So it's crays for now.

Anyway.

Old Ben lives alone, unless you count his son's dingo-kelpie cross, Bazza—still pining for his long-lost master—and the hundred ewes and free-range chickens he runs for their eggs and meat.

Mrs Lyons died of cancer, Ben told us, way before we were born.

His only son, the "Wildcat" Lyons, used the shed to store his diving gear, his fishing nets, a punch bag with two sets of gloves and bits and pieces for the tinny, until a roadside bomb on a track in Uruzgan province in Afghanistan went off and killed him in 2019.

Old Ben's been travelling solo ever since.

He's always stoked to see us.

So is Bazza. Whenever we launch the tinny he's the first aboard, balancing on the foredeck and barking at the seagulls, like he's Captain Cook thinking all his Christmases have come at once when he landed on our empty continent in Botany Bay and ignored the Gweagal welcoming party that told him to piss off.

We often use the punch bag when the testosterone is working up our aggression and we want to let off steam, and we use the gloves with Mozzie to keep him fit in the ring we made with star pickets and a rope. Mozzie's happiest when he's taking one of us on. His straight left is so lightning-quick you never see it coming. Our occasional black eyes can vouch for that.

"Bones" Scully was the bruh who came across the shack two years ago when we were still thirteen. He's our middle-distance runner, with so much potential Athletics Australia have got their eye on him. He was with his folks in the Lucky Bay campsite one weekend when he took a morning run through the dunes. He turned round at the shack when he came across it, checked it out and reported back to us at school first thing Monday morning.

He was amped.

We were in the GG Boarders' College dining room about to eat breakfast. "You won't believe this," he burst out. "I've found what we've been looking for. A shack. It's the bee's knees."

"The bee's knees?" Mozzie asked. "What language is that? Pom?"

"It's perfect."

"You mean it's fire?"

"You bet. It's really lit!"

"That's better."

He had scrawled a map of the beach, pinpointing with a cross where he figured it was, like some sort of treasure map.

Tiny reached across and took it.

No one argued with Tiny. He'd turned fifteen, drove an off-road Jeep Wrangler and was already built like a brick shithouse. Not having a driver's licence wasn't a problem. His stepfather owned a property at Howatharra and Tiny knew all the back roads through the farming country from there. The few times he did take to the main roads it was usually at night, sometimes with the lights out. He hasn't been stopped yet. Maybe the traffic cops thought he was a man and gave him the benefit of the doubt, he was that big. Whatever the case, he was a wizard and could get us anywhere.

He may not have been an Alpha like the rest us, but he was definitely a Sigma, and we followed him. No one knew why he lined himself up with us, all two years younger than him, but we weren't complaining. We had protection and above all, wheels.

We've never heard him mention it and we'll never ask, but everyone knows his dad, Uncle Jimmy, died when Tiny was four—in the back of the paddy wagon when they were driving him to the Casuarina Prison in Perth. Accidental heat stroke when the aircon broke down, they said, so no one got the blame. His dad was up for aggravated assault, when he took on some white bloke on Red Hill Station. He was a Yingkarta Yamaji man from the Gascoyne, so Tiny's one of our mob.

"Looks like it's on the Lyons's land," he said. "Old Ben lives there. I knew his son, the Wildcat. I'll drop in and have a yarn."

Two weeks later the shack was ours.

Old Ben even gave us a name plate to hang above the door. The "Lyons Den" it read, burned with a welder's flame across a knotty piece of pine.

He allows us to come and go as we please, which is mostly at the weekends when we get off school, or during the holidays. To return the favour, some nights we make a point of keeping him company or invite him to the Den, and we always bog in and lend a hand when he needs something done.

He's a bony old bloke, burned brown by a lifetime in the sun. He's one of those old Aussie vets so full of life you'd never guess their age. Take his eyes. They're bright blue and piercing, with a cheeky glint to them now and then, like he's seen the funny side of one of our jokes. He shaves his hair to a crewcut, but lets his eyebrows grow any way they please and gazes out from under them like he's looking way into the distance. He wears his faithful grey Akubra hat everywhere, even indoors. With its stained and bendy brim and holes in its crown it looks like it's growing out the top of his head and has to be as old as he is. All his shirts are blue or red check, so thin from years of laundering away his sweat you can almost see his ribs through their cotton weave. We always know what to buy him on his birthday, and it's not a hat.

"I'd only be long in the tooth," he told us one night, when he was sitting with us round the campfire at the shack and Mozzie asked him how old he was, "if I had any. Watch this."

And he spat his shiny pink upper dentures into an empty tin bucket a metre away.

"Now you try that when you get to my age. Which is a lot older than you're guessing."

I kid you not.

We saw him do it.

So did Willie Mack. "So that's the cost of living, Ben," he commented thoughtfully.

"The what?" Ben asked.

"The cost of living."

"What is?"

"Growing old." Willie Mack said.

"And then you die," Ben replied at once. "There's always a price to pay. You should know that by now." Then he thought for a moment, before adding, "There is one compensation, though."

"What's that?" Willie Mack asked.

"You're always younger than you think you are, because you're never quite as old as you're gunna get. Yep. You can look forward to those memories that haven't happened yet that you're gunna enjoy looking back on when you're older. Like me tonight tomorrow, boys." He held out his right arm and shook the flap of empty skin below his shoulder where his triceps used to be. "That's when you'll wear your skin loose like I do, because it's more comfortable that way. Trust me."

"Can't fault that logic." Willie Mack smiled.

"Too right. I like to call a spade a fucking shovel," Ben said. "You boys should learn to do the same."

The old bloke had lost the rest of us, though. We smiled vaguely at him as we wondered what the hell he was going on about.

The shack is the perfect meeting place.

We have all the infrastructure we need.

An old generator bruh "Spanner" O'Toole takes care of.

A forty-four-gallon drum we fill with water when we visit, tilted at an angle with a tap at its lower end.

A solar heated shower with its tank up on the roof.

A two-seater long-drop dunny with an inland view across Route 139, George Grey Drive, and up into the hills. It's a two-seater, in case. If someone else wants to drop a load the same time as you, at least you've got someone to talk to. And it has a view to die for. You can count the passing cars to offset the boredom when you're taking a dump. And we keep a full can of Mortein on the seat to shoot down the blowies when they're flying in formation and putting on a show, like the Blue Angels in the USAF.

A four-legged barbecue plate two metres long and one across, with a handle on it indicating it was once a door for who knows what.

Inside, it has two rooms and it's much the same with the furnishings.

Adequate, which in our eyes means luxurious.

A front room for starters, with a beanbag each, and our Hexagonal Table. It's a top job. Tiny made it in the Cabinet Maker's workshop from a smashed-up jarrah sideboard we recovered from the roadside collection. And we have six cane chairs inherited from Wildcat. They're so old you have to be careful when you sit so you don't get spiked. Tiny has to take care anyway. He has to adjust his *kuca* to avoid sitting on one because they're big as grapefruit.

And a bedroom, with two double bunks that were also Wildcat's, and now one foldable foam mattress on the floor, not two, with Mozzie gone.

That's us.

We're the Alpha Bruhs of the Hexagonal Table, inaugurated in December 2022. We've got each other's backs, finding our thorny horny way through teenage hood on the journey to becoming men. Or so we think, without quite saying so. It's our unspoken aim that sort of morphed that way, with a single rule and a national anthem to seal the deal.

So, how did it all start?

Well. Mid-October 2022. We're living in Matthew Flinders House in the school's GG Boarders' College and playing cards together in the Common Room most evenings. Pontoon sometimes, for plastic tokens the school provides, but mostly euchre for the fun of it, and the competitiveness.

It's that time towards the end of term, with Covid lockdowns a thing of the past—"No more Covid lockdowns!" was Willie Mack's comment last year. "That's not to be sneezed at!"—but the unfair four-year ban on crayfish exports to China is still firmly in place.

Mozzie and Tiny's parents are pissed as hell about that. They have a living to make and crayboats to maintain. Which means that Tiny has access to his stepdad's *Quixote II* now and again when she needs a run.

"She's a forty-foot Millman jetboat built in 1978," he tells us one evening. "She may be old, but her engine's new. She goes like the clappers and turns on a five-cent piece. You guys want to come out for a ride?"

He asks for another card, grins, and then slaps down three sevens and casually scrapes in the bank. It's a Royal Pontoon that wins the house, and we've never seen one before.

Our luck must be in.

Touch wood.

"It's the Spring by the Sea Festival next week," he goes on. "*Iwarra Wilungga*, all for a good cause. My stepdad's crook so I'm taking her out to give people a spin. I'll need a crew to man the boat and give the passengers a good time. Not to mention collect the takings for the Primary Health mob."

Five of us pipe up at once, so quickly you can't tell who said what.

"My bloody oath!"

"You bet!"

"I'm in!"

"Are you kidding?"

"Me too!"

We help him with the clean-up and the decorations in the evenings of that week. Nothing flash, with a name like *Quixote II*. Some black, red and yellow streamers hanging from the headlight and the aerials is all. For the Nicholson's *Salty Miss*, the only other boat taking part, it's a different matter. On the Saturday afternoon she's dressed up like she's going to a ball, but we still beat their takings by half again.

The music on the shore isn't bad. Red Ochre. Born2Sing. And the newbies from Perth, South Summit. We haven't heard them before. They are Mozzie's favourite from the get-go for their rock, reggae and hip-hop mix, but none of the rest us get off on them at the time. Not country rock enough for us. We get to like them later though, once we get used to them. Like them a lot.

On the Sunday after that we're out among the Abrolhos Islands, Spanner heaving over the side on the way across, showing us what he's made of. For most of the trip. It's a wonder when we get there that there's any of him left. Which is ironic, because he's the crazy fisherman among us— bottom fishing, trolling, ballooning, you name it, he can't get enough of it. He has a collection of rods and reels second to none. When he starts on about it you can't shut him up. He bores you shitless and clears the room.

Sixty kilometres. It takes us three hours, with Tiny on cruise control to save diesel.

Mozzie's the only one wearing a lifejacket too big for him. He's never been out on a crayboat before—even though his dad owns one—and he's not the swimmer we are. He has these two phobias. He can't stand heights, even if it's only two stories up, and he isn't keen on the water. Boxing's his thing. And Maths and Science. He's high key at all three.

I can vouch for that.

We hook a small Longtail on the way for bait, and when we get there drop the bottom lines off Plover Island for a Coral Trout or two for dinner. We troll for Spanish mackas or Yellowfin on the way back in, without a hit.

It's our first experience as Alpha Bruhs and we can feel the glue that's gunna bind us for the next two years beginning to do its thing. Sticking us together tighter than a tube of Araldite. Tight as a snake's you know what.

It's not the sun and windburn.

It's the real thing.

And we know it's gunna last.

Still under the spell of the weekend before, we talk about it on Monday evening in the Common Room. We have it to ourselves for once. We stretch our legs out on a borrowed chair. Nowadays we have the Wellness Room which would have suited us then, but that was still two years away.

"We're onto a good thing here," Tiny says, his hands behind his head "I don't mean the friendship we share. I mean the GG Boarders' College. We're well looked after. All our needs are taken care of."

"Yeah, right down to the semolina pudding," Bones says.

We all look across at Willie Mack and laugh.

Semolina was new on the menu a week ago.

"What's this? Rat poison?" Larry Perkins asked, looking down at his plate.

"If *you* survive it," Willie Mack roasted him as he took a second helping, "we'll know it's not."

"*Smartarse!*" Larry says as he storms away.

"We couldn't be better off," Tiny goes on. "The staff are okay. Beats having your old folks hanging around. Excursions. A swimming pool to die for."

Willie Mack chuckles at that. "Talking of swimming pools to die for, why didn't the bloke who was drowning in one realise he was drowning?"

"Why?" Spanner asks.

"Because it didn't sink in."

Spanner groans, gets up and punches him on the shoulder. Twice. It's the new punishment we dish out to anyone who's made a booboo. We call it "giving a blue-bean" because of the size, shape and colour of the bruise it leaves. We prefer that to the sack tap, where your nut bag cops a hit. One of the boys in Matthew Flinders House before our time got a swollen testicle bigger than Tiny's after a sack tap and they had to remove it. Everyone called him "Hitler" after that. One ball Hitler. Or so the rumours go.

I'm not sure who first started the blue-bean practice or where he got the name from. It sounds Baby Boomer to me, but that's okay. One if it's forgivable. Two if it's so-so. And three if it's a howler. Believe me, we make the punches count. We're full of testosterone, don't forget. Especially Bones and Spanner.

Spanner even gets a hard-on when he's sitting in a car from the vibrations in the passenger seat. We've seen the way he walks when he gets out. It doesn't last, though, because we tease him every time. His "Hey, you guys, cut it out!" is very sheepish and Willie Mack's "We may have to," doesn't go down too well.

Tiny takes no notice. "We have a simple three-word code of conduct in the boarding house here," he goes on. "Respectful. Responsible. Caring. They all matter, of course they do. And they suit the girls in Edith Cowan House. But we need more. Something with edge. Something with fire."

"A quest, you mean. Like the Knights of the Round Table?" Mozzie asks. "All equal and looking for the Holy Grail?"

"Nothing quite so Pommie and mediaeval," Willie Mack says. "Something more Aussie."

"A band of brothers?" I suggest.

"That's closer. We're all Alpha gens, except for you Tiny, but we'll allow for that. So how does Alpha Bruhs sound?" Willie Mack asks.

"And there's six of us, don't forget." Bones looks up from the latest *Runners' World Annual* he's reading. "That makes our table hexagonal, not round," he adds, before looking back at the page he's reached.

"Great idea," Tiny says. "I'll make it. No dramas."

Tiny is our gun carpenter. He already works in his spare time in the 'Cabinet Makers' workshop, recently opened in Beresford.

"The Alpha Bruhs of the Hexagonal Table. I like it," I say. "It has a nice sound to it, like it really means something."

Which it does.

And so the band of brothers was born.

Chapter 4

WHEN I HIT THE sack at night I like to read before I drop off. For an hour or so, while I charge my mobile phone and get my breath back after a day of school. Sometimes I turn to the previous entries in my Dreaming exercise books, to refresh my memory and think about the possibilities of what they mean.

Some are strange. Really, really strange.

Yours too?

Then I guess we both know what I mean.

Take this one I had in July 2020, after the snake dream.

I had it just the once, during the night on Friday, February 14. On Valentine's Day night of all nights.

You expecting something sexy? You wish. I was still only ten.

Cop this.

I'm on a beach somewhere in the Indian Ocean, at the edge of a protected bay.

I know it's the Indian Ocean because I'm watching two dark brown boys wearing loincloths, who wouldn't look out of place among us Yamaji mob except for the clothes. Somehow, I know they're brothers. They're playing on the sand. Soccer, it seems, kicking what looks like a dry old coconut. One's about my age at ten, the other's four years older, give or take.

There's a long jetty to my right.

It has a black stone pipeline running its length. Each metre-long stone is tightly connected to the next, and I see it runs up the steep hillside behind me, disappearing among densely packed palm trees. Cackling bright green parakeets with red and yellow beaks and long blue tails are fluttering here and there among their fronds.

At the end of the jetty there's a flat-bottomed boat about twenty metres long. Painted sky blue with a strange black eyeball at the bow. Looking out for rocks, I guess. It has a forward sloping mast and a lowered sail like I've never seen before.

There's a bloke in the boat wearing a loincloth round his waist and the same around his head, filling seven wooden barrels in his boat with what must be water pouring from the pipe.

Beyond the jetty there's a causeway curving round to a solid stone fort on a rocky promontory. Is that a Dutch flag flying from the battlements? *Orange*, white and blue stripes? It would be if the orange was red, like I learned in Civics and Citizenship.

Beyond that lies the ocean like an open invitation.

You get the picture? Where are we do you reckon? India? Sri Lanka? Not the Maldives, they're flat. The Seychelles, maybe.

Your guess is as good as mine.

Then I check out the bay and get a shock.

That three masted ship again.

A ghost ship?

Who knows?

Maybe not, because it's much closer this time, so close I can see the cannons and the shadows of people working on the decks.

I hear the old man's shout, see him wave, and both boys sprint towards him.

I see he's shut down the flow of water.

So, I'm a spectator in this dream. One of the chat. With a bird's eye view over everything.

The older boy raises the sail. It's triangular and attached to a pole that arches out beyond the bow and close to the stern. When the sail fills, the boat skims across to the ship in no time flat.

It ties up alongside and sailors on the mid deck open up a gate in the rail. They lower a net attached to a rope and the two boys roll a single barrel into it.

I find it interesting to watch.

Even though I'm a spectator, I can feel the hot deck under my bare feet, can hear the cracking twang of the rope as it tightens and am deafened by the chanting of the five sailors straining as they turn the capstan, until the first barrel scrapes over the side and onto the deck.

A sailor rolls it away and the procedure's repeated six more times.

When the barrels are stowed away, well, it turns out that's when the fun starts.

The sailors gather at the rail as the man in the boat unties the stern line.

The wind or tide slowly swings the boat away from the ship, and as it turns the two boys dive into the sunlit water. They both look up, all white teeth as they grin. They're wearing crude wooden goggles like John Lennon granny glasses, bound with a cloth tied tight over their ears and around the back of their heads.

A sailor tosses them a silver coin.

Out of reach.

The younger boy dives, legs thrashing.

He follows as it flickers this way and that like a bright-lit fishing spinner before he retrieves it three metres down. Then he surfaces and, still grinning, waves the coin as his brother dives deeper for another. He puts the coin in his mouth, and you can see him push it into his cheek with his tongue before he dives again as his brother surfaces.

Several coins later, the man in the boat, with his foot now on the foredeck, murmurs something I can't hear to the boys with bulging cheeks and stretches up to loosen the bow line.

A final coin, a gold one this time, splashes in behind them.

They both dive for it.

It's already deep as they race to reach it, the younger boy turning for the surface part way down. I feel the older boy's ears bursting as he loops upside down beneath it, catches it in both hands and swims to the surface.

He bursts from the water and waves the coin, which he puts in his mouth.

He's shaking the water from his hair and his brother is tilting his goggles to empty them when a gigantic shadow passes through the space the older boy would have reached with another downward stroke.

The sailors scream.

The man in the boat shouts and reaches for a boathook.

Neither boy can hear them through the binding of the goggles as the shark makes a second pass. The pressure of its glide thrusts the younger boy's legs sideways as the older boy looks up. He sees the sailors waving wildly and glimpses the man in the boat shouting as he runs across the boat with the boathook.

The younger boy brings his knees to his chest and sinks below the older boy as the man in the boat hurls the boathook deep into the water between them.

Missed!

He's no Queequeg.

The older boy tears the cloth from his ears and tosses the goggles aside. He hears the yelling, spits out his coins, and is shocked to see the pandemonium on the deck as the younger boy thrashes his way to safety, clambering over him and sobbing.

The older boy grips the younger firmly with his left hand.

He ducks beneath the surface as the shark glides across his front.

Although his sight is blurred, he sees the membrane sweep in slow motion across the cold and empty lens of its eye, black and saucer-sized, before the immense barred body sweeps past, tapering to a broad nicked tail that flicks his brother's legs and the blood pours.

Then the shark, with its wide square nose and tan bars lit along its flanks, turns to come directly at the thrashing boys, charging in from the ship's bow.

The older boy catches the boathook that has floated up behind him.

He struggles to pull it through the water's resistance to face the shark he can no longer see.

He holds his other arm around his younger brother, gripping his armpit as the shark makes a direct charge at them both.

Its tail churns the surface and the boathook passes harmlessly over its head.

The older boy is blinded underwater as the jaws tear into his younger brother, taking both boys into the side of the ship.

And then the shark, head shaking and great body thrashing and twisting, tows them out of the ship's shadow and into the sunlit water at the bow. There the blood spreads like crimson smoke and the older boy feels his brother's body lighten as the shark tears itself away.

The older boy hauls his brother to the hawser of the ship's forward anchor where he hangs on with his right hand. I can feel his horror as he finds himself clutching his younger brother's upper torso with his left, his head lolling and a silver waterfall of glittering coins bursting from his open mouth.

From the upper decks, the seamen watch helplessly as the shark circles again, the boy's severed lower abdomen and legs entangled in its dislocating jaw, held there by knots of intestines it struggles to disgorge.

It dives slowly from sight, trailing clouds of blood and the streaming russet of the young boy's loincloth.

The older boy struggles to climb out of the water and up the rope, hanging on to his brother's wrist, but the weight and steep angle are too much for him.

His arms numb, he hangs there, groaning, until he lets his brother go,

He watches the man in the boat retrieve the torso before it sinks.

He looks down and sees his bleeding ribs exposed, his skin ripped open up his chest when the shark brushed past him.

Shocked, he climbs the rope to the wooden carving of the lion at the bow.

He clasps it, shivering and moaning, until two sailors clamber down towards him.

That's when I force myself to wake. I struggle back to consciousness, panicked and feeling sick, as if I'm waiting for the credits to roll for a horror movie I haven't enjoyed.

When I describe the dream to Mum and Dad, she's the one who gives me the answer.

With no hesitation.

"That's Jurien Bay!" she says. "When Mum and Dad were living there. They used to talk about it. In the mid-nineteen-sixties, it was. Bobby Bartle and Lee Warner. Weren't they spearfishing for Jewies over half a kilometre out, when Bobby got hit by a Great White and torn in half? I'm sure that's the way it happened. Lee swam ashore to get help. Do you remember, Alan?"

"Vaguely," Dad replies. "Rings a bell. I don't think I ever heard the full story. Did Lee bring Bobby's top half ashore?"

"I don't think so."

Mum turns back to me. "You're amazing, Suma. I don't know where you're getting your vibes from."

"Must be AI," Dad says drily, as he does. Like I say, he takes some getting used to and I usually come off second best. "You couldn't have dreamed that up yourself."

Sometimes I feel so rejected by his scorn I hate him for throwing shade on most of the things I do. I have never shown him my pastel drawings for that reason. Their colours speak to me. I like to blend them, making colours that are mine and mine alone, but I keep them to myself.

Have I foretold the past again? I wonder. Bobby Bartle and Lee Warner? That's another one to google. Were they Indian or Sri Lankan? Was it three hundred years ago? Was there a wooden three-masted ship in Jurien Bay? I don't think so.

Chapter 5

The Lyons Den, Saturday, 10 December, 2022. End of term.

I'LL NEVER FORGET THE first time we gathered round the Hexagonal Table in the Lyons Den, officially, formally, as if we were a committee in council.

We sat smiling at one another for half a minute, conscious it was a pivotal moment in our lives we'd never forget.

Willie Mack agreed to take the minutes.

Then, without any prompting, Bones started the proceedings.

On the wrong foot.

"There's something in the air tonight," he sang, his voice flat as usual. "And I can feel it coming in the air tonight, Oh Lord!" Before he farted loud and long.

"Bloody Bones! You and your backchat! You blowing your own trumpet again?" Willie Mack shouted. "That one would have turned a windmill."

He earned three blue-beans for his effort, delivered by Tiny so they really counted as we exited the room with our wicker chairs and decided to sit around the barbecue fire instead. Except for Bones, there wasn't much wind that night. Even the flames on the fire were small and virtually still, the embers glowing.

Bloody Bones!

He told us one day his dad had traced his ancestry back to a first fleet convict in 1788.

"Your dad's right," Tiny said. "We can tell that by looking at you."

"That's not *my* fault," Bones replied, giving Tiny that crooked, unsure smile he's got. "Want me to teach you how to pick someone's pocket? That's what my six times great-grandad Billy Scully was transported out from London for.

One silver sovereign, so the records say. And here I am."

He's full of wind, but that's okay.

He's one of us.

Except when he lets one go.

"For starters, we need some sort of initiation ceremony," Tiny said. "Something that's gunna bind us as a group—and individually let us know we're on our way to becoming teenagers who know how to become men."

"I've already been circumcised," Mozzie said, "If that's what you mean."

I looked at Willie Mack, frowned and shook my head in case he was about to come out with: "Yes. We've noticed. That explains why it's so small. I was bigger than that when I was ten." But he didn't. He was more understanding than that, especially with Mozzie and his phobias.

"Something similar," Tiny said. "Something painful that leaves a mark. So you bear the pain and wear the consequences. Like a badge of honour. Know what I mean?"

"Like the Cobras, Ace and Eyeball, in *Stand By Me*?" Bones asked. "Remember that movie?"

"Pretty much," Tiny said. "Something like that."

"I saw a documentary about that last month!" Mozzie was suddenly amped. "The Crocodile Men of the East Sepik or some such title. It was so interesting. It's an ancient tradition. They carve the backs and bums of the blokes getting initiated with small triangular cuts over a couple of months, so the scars look like the scales of a croc. I'm talking *cuts*. Deep ones. With a scalpel. Or a piece of glass. There was blood everywhere. Buckets of it. After that you know you're a man. It's a kind of power mark that keeps you connected to your ancestors. In their case, that is. It keeps the culture alive. Links you to your totem, or whatever."

As I mentioned, Mozzie is our Maths and Science nerd. He's goated at both. He's a fan of Brian Cox. He's always travelling round the universe with him. His parents have already booked a room in the Potshot Hotel Resort in Exmouth for a week next April to watch the sun's eclipse. Mozzie can't wait. He's wetting his pants at the thought of the sun going out.

"What about a proper tatt?" Willie Mack asked. "Wouldn't that do the trick?"

"Sure it would, but good luck with that. You try it," Spanner said. "You won't get far. I wanted one and found out it's illegal. I checked with the blokes in Skin Magic Tatts. They said they can't give you one till you're eighteen. Or you need one for medical reasons. Even then you've got Buckley's without a doctor's say so. If a tatts parlour gives you one they're up before the magistrate, they said. They wouldn't risk it. Not even when I doubled the money."

"So?" Willie Mack said. "We give up on the idea? *No!* We come up with an alternative. We think outside the box. Old Twiga keeps telling to do that in English class, doesn't he?"

"Like you did last year, Willie?" I asked.

"Like I did *what* last year?"

"Thought outside the box."

"When was that exactly?"

"When he asked us to write that essay. The one about what we wanted to be when we grow up. You wrote about becoming a dodo taxidermist," I smiled. "That essay ate, bruh. It was right outside the box."

"Oh yeah, I remember that. He got so pissed off he made me write another one, so I wrote about becoming a Scuba diver working as a plumber on a Sewage Farm. With a side business growing tomatoes from the seedlings that pop up there. That one he saw the funny side of, the old fart. Probably thought he wouldn't mind the plumber's job himself... and prefers tomatoes on the vine, no matter where the seeds come from. Beats teaching."

Twiga Gammie had a soft spot for Willie Mack. He'd lift one crutch and point it at Willie when the rest of us were sitting there in stunned silence without an answer to a question. "What about you Mr William Wordsmith, our poet of the twenty first century?" he'd ask. "Do *you* have the answer? I hope so, because the rest of these geniuses are having trouble expressing themselves. Must be because they think they're too clever for words."

He still has his Kenya accent, like he's an Afrikaner.

I'll never forget the first time he used his crutch as a snooker cue, during the second lesson he ever took with us. He steadied himself, aimed and then tapped the back of Spanner's head with the rubber tip. Hard. Spanner had been whispering to Bones and didn't see it coming, but we did and held our breath.

Isn't he breaking the law? I remember thinking but didn't say so. *Isn't that aggravated assault?*

"The House of Reason," Twiga growled. "Untenanted, naturally, and up for lease. The curtains are open but nobody's home. Next time I knock to enquire it will be twice as loud. What's your name, boy?"

He'd got the message across to us, loud and clear.

Anyway.

"We do it our bloody selves," Spanner broke in. "How's that, for starters? That'd work!"

"Right on the money," Tiny said. "Good one Spanner. That's a triple seven, right there. We do it ourselves in a spot that's not too noticeable. After plenty of practice. On a piece of pigskin or fake skin. We have to get the gear and learn to use it. Are we all agreed?"

"Sounds good to me."

"No dramas."

"Bloody oath."

"As long as the secret spot is not my dick."

"Or my *manda*."

Tiny looked across at Willie Mack. "You're the secretary and treasurer, Willie. Take that down. Google the kit. We'll have a collection. Whatever you can spare. We'll troll the internet and order one in. Now we need the design."

"Easy," Bones said. "You've made the table. We've sat around it. The tatt has to be a hexagon."

"Of course it does," Tiny said. "Plain and simple."

"What about AB in the centre. For Alpha Bruhs," Mozzie asked.

Tiny thought for a moment. "Too complicated. Those for?"

Two hands went up, then one was quickly withdrawn.

"The no's have it." Tiny said. "We keep it small and plain. Maybe shaded in with your favourite colour."

"What about a different colour each? That would make us individuals, but still one of the bruhs," Bones suggested.

"What if two of us want the same colour? We get the boxing gloves out?" Mozzie asked.

"Then the loser ends up with a colour he doesn't want," I said.

"Good point, Summer. We choose our own colours or leave it plain if you prefer. Now think about where we want it," Tiny said. After a short silence he went on, "We can decide that later. No good running before we can walk."

He looked around the group. Willie Mack was back into the shack. We could see him at the table scribbling into his ring-bound notebook.

"Anyone got anything to add?" Tiny asked. "No? Then this first meeting is adjourned. Well done boys. Time for refreshments and some Coral Trout or Bluebone. Who's the chef tonight? You, Mozzie? Thanks. Hey, Spanner, there's some Cokes on ice in the esky and a can of Rocky Ridge Draught each I snuck from my stepdad for those who fancy tasting something stronger. Just for tasting, bruhs. It's never gunna be piss up time in the Lyons Den. Think that and you're banned. For good. It's not what we're here for. Agreed?"

"Sounds fair to me."

"No problem."

"Too right."

"Suits me."

"Me too," Willie Mack shouts from inside the shack.

"Doesn't mean we can't have a *taste* now and then." Tiny said. "I think that's fair after a hard day's sweat. And it's always good to get to know what we're up against. What I'm saying is we don't get fired up and pissed because no one's looking. That's when you find out what sort of a man you really are. When you've got no witnesses."

He sat back, put his feet up on a rock and took a long choof from his vape.

"Same goes for drugs," he said. "We all know what Geraldton is famous for."

I could see him thinking, *Job well done. The tribe has spoken. We're on our way*

Then I thought some more about it and something that had puzzled me for some time fell into place.

It's always good to get to know what we're up against, Tiny had said, and I realised, *He must mean his white stepfather. Drunk, and fighting with his Yamaji mother now and then, like he's affected by the full moon once a month and can't resist the turps. He told us about the time he had to step in and stop him beating up his Mum one night last year. Past midnight. In their bedroom. Going at it, like she was a punching bag backed up against the dressing table, knocking over the scent bottles and smashing the hand mirror, screaming like a feral cat as she tried to give as good as she was getting, but coming off second best. Until Tiny appeared at the door, swinging his stepfather's number one wood driver he'd lifted from the golf bag when he'd woken up and couldn't stand the row. That quietened them down, leaving Tiny shaking. It wasn't like that all the time, he told us. At other times his stepfather was okay. Just not his real father, who we knew had died in the paddy wagon when he was four.*

I stood to get a plate of Mozzie's crayfish and a fillet of Coral Trout and salad, took a Coke from the esky and sat back down.

So that's where Tiny's coming from, I realised. He's our guide, the guide he hasn't got himself. Our guardian and protector.

I took a long drag from the Coke.

I don't mind following his lead. We share the same problems with our Dads, him and me—but in my case without the physical violence it's a different sort of war.

Chapter 6

If I came close to that wooden ship in the bay when the shark attack occurred in one dream, I came closer in another in January last year.

I re-read it last night.

It starts off on a calm day under a clear blue sky.

It's mid-Summer maybe? Sometime in July, perhaps.

I'm a participant this time. At first, that is. Then I'm also able to take in the scene as an eyeball in the sky.

Weird.

So, I'm walking with a crowd of strangely dressed people along a canal in a town I can't name. Two windmills we pass tell me its somewhere in the Netherlands.

It must be three or four hundred years ago, at a guess. Long dresses and bonnets on the women. Black pointy hats, frilled collars and black suits on the men. They don't know I'm there, or if they do they couldn't care less.

Which suits me fine.

They're billowing pipe smoke like a bushfire. The stink of burning tobacco is choking, but they don't seem to care. Just take another choof, tilt back their heads and let a long stream of grey smoke curl up from both nostrils. The men mostly. Some women. They're talking in a language that sounds pig gibberish to me. It's loud and exuberant. There's laughter too, filling the air with excitement, like something insane is about to happen, to be honest.

Like Bazza, they're thinking all their Christmases are coming at once.

Then I get a bird's eye view and I'm shocked.

There she is, up ahead on the canal.

My ghost ship.

Sails furled.

I see a double row of windows in her intricately carved high-rising stern, six below and four above. Eight yellow carvings like gargoyles are fixed across her beam below the windows.

There's a name painted across the upper timbers I can barely make out.

It's the *Zuiddorp*!

Not the *Zuytdorp*, the way Uncle Lennard spelt it for me. That must be the Australian version.

I hadn't noticed the name in the previous dream.

Four powerful white and black dappled carthorses, two on each bank, are towing her towards the town. The muscles in their giant round rumps quiver with every stride as they strain against the rope harnesses, and a bloke in a red coat with polished boots to match is putting on a show. He's waving a long-poled whip and cracking the leather in the air like he's a circus ringmaster, before landing one on a horse's backside, the dappled skin twitching madly like the horse is getting rid of March flies.

The crowds cheer him on.

Then one of the horses on the near side reacts to one of his whip strokes by lifting its tail, baring its brown spot to the crowd and letting go a steaming jet of khaki shit at three young women with their hands around their waists following too closely behind.

That's sweet revenge, I think, *great to watch*, as the women disengage, do a quick sidestep, hop over the pile and kick up their legs as if they're practising a can-can routine to clear the muck from their shoes.

Up ahead the canal leads to an inner harbour. The wide expanse of water is surrounded by tightly packed three-storey buildings. On the far bank I see the entrances to three other canals leading from the harbour into the town that's closer now, a single grey church spire sticking up several stories high in the centre.

There are two longboats on the water in the harbour, each with eight oarsmen holding their gleaming wet blades upright. They're obviously waiting to take over from the horses and tow the ship to its quayside destination.

I follow the crowd across a bridge and into the town. Or city. Tall red and white brick buildings line the streets, three stories high and packed close together, each with a fancy flat stonework front triangulating up to a point beneath the roof. We walk down narrow cobbled laneways with the faint stink of piss, until the brief strong smell of raw coffee surprises me as we pass.

People everywhere.

Girls chasing hoops.

Boys kicking balls.

Snarling dogs going at it in a three-way fight, lips drawn back, teeth bared.

A black and then a mangy ginger cat slinking out of sight.

It's what?

It's pandemonium.

That's the word describes it.

I've used it before; in case it surprised you this time. Maybe Twiga Gammie's influence is rubbing off after all.

About time.

Then we reach another wide canal curving round to the right and disappearing among the buildings. Three gliding yellow-beaked white swans. Several scooting black moorhens leaving tracks on the water before diving bum up for an underwater peek.

Two towering three-masted ships are moored alongside, their ropes attached to bollards. The *Belvliet*, I read on the stern of the first. The *Vaderland Getrouw* on the other. Beside each is a tall tripod that must be a crane.

There are warehouses beside them. I read the names on boards above the upper windows as I pass: *De Kameel*. The

Camel? *De Geit.* No idea. The Goat, maybe? I breathe the strong smell of spices now, like Mum's kitchen pantry. Pepper. Nutmeg. Maybe cloves or cinnamon, I don't know. My nose threatens to start running so I move away, closer to the ships.

Then we stop at *De Olifant.* That has to be the Elephant, where my ghost ship towed by the two rowing boats is floating in mid canal.

Her mooring ropes are attached to the bollards, and I can hear the crew on board at the deck capstans singing and stamping their feet as they winch her alongside, as they did when they were lifting the water barrels in the other dream

The decks sweep away above me, a line of faces at the rail.

As she moves closer, one mad sailor clambers onto the rail. With a warning scream he hurls himself across the narrowing gap between the ship and the quay. People part, and he lands, overbalances, and somersaults into the crowd, where he lies kissing the quayside brickwork.

The crowd roars.

A second figure and then a third follow him, hanging outstretched in mid-air before falling to the bricks.

And then shock settles in my gut like I've swallowed ground glass.

Among the faces above me, I see someone who looks like an Indian.

The boy who survived the shark attack?

Surely not!

He's carrying a brilliant green parakeet, a loose drawstring connecting its leg to his wrist. It's exactly like those I saw at the beach among the palm trees in the other dream. Its red beak's tipped with yellow and it has the same long blue tail.

It has to be him!

There's a young bloke standing next to me who nods at the Indian, and he nods in return.

I take a closer look at him. He's wearing a grey felt hat with a wide brim, splashed with paint and tar. He takes it off and runs his fingers through his spiky hair, which looks as if it's regrown after being recently shaved off. The parakeet flaps and shrieks in alarm.

Then he disappears.

Fifteen minutes later I see him coming down the bouncing gangway. He's shouldering what looks like a black canvas swag and carrying the parakeet in a bamboo cage. He's following a bloke togged out like an officer. Very smart. Blue coat to his knees. Silver buttons all the way down. White trousers, bell bottoms. Very blond longish hair, almost ash. Sharp blue eyes. Long nose. Clean shaven. Sunburned hawkish no-nonsense face. Weathered look, with peeling lips now he's closer.

You know what I mean.

They step ashore, and the officer introduces the Indian to the young bloke who was standing beside me.

I know it's him now. Just a slightly older version. Fifteen, maybe. The same dark eyes I remember. Not quite as innocent as they were, but as sincere. More experienced. Confident, but reserved at the same time. It's like someone I've known in the distant past and missed for years has walked back into my life.

Then the bloke standing next to me separates and goes up the gangway, while the other two disappear into the crowd, leaving me wondering what happened.

I don't have the time or inclination to walk to the ship's stern and check the name again, because it's as if the dream has fast forwarded and I see the Indian and the young bloke riding horses outside the city.

It's a windy early morning, a week later.

A week? How do I know? Don't ask me. I'm the spectator, not the projectionist. Unless there really is a sky-pilot at the controls in my sleeping brain and never mind Willie Mack's scepticism.

They pass what looks like a grain silo, where two girls in red uniforms are whistling at a pack of yapping terriers clearly chasing rats. One of them turns and waves at the young bloke, who takes off his scarlet scarf and waves it back at her.

They follow a track towards the north.

The wind keeps catching the brim of the Indian's hat, pushing it down over his face. It blinds him, but protects him from passing jet-propelled bumblebees as the odd one riding on the wind slaps into his face but hits the brim.

Splat!

They cross wooden bridges, the horses stumbling, over irrigation channels across wide green fields of what? Is that tobacco? Looks like it. The tall red-green tops of beetroot? Perhaps. The maize I recognise.

There are whitewashed farmhouses here and there, sheltered among pointy cypress trees, their dense green foliage spiralling upwards.

In one field a farmer's ploughing furrows behind a team of oxen. I can see flocks of wagtails flitting across the field to check out the black soil for worms or beetles as it turns.

When they pass through the next small town there's a deafening explosion. The horses rear up and skitter backwards. The Indian clutches his horse's mane as he slides off. A cannon shot? I can hear it still reverberating. It must be midday and that's the signal. The young bloke's not concerned and the Indian remounts.

When they reach the next town on the coast, they stop at a tavern beside a steep-sided dune.

It's like I'm back in the Lyons Den at Lucky Bay.

They drink from brown bottles in the garden, sitting on a bench built around the trunk of a huge and shady tree. The wind is stronger now and I can hear the splash of the sea rolling up the sand beyond the dunes. The faint familiar smell of drying seaweed tells me there's an outgoing tide.

They refill their bottles and the young bloke stows them in his saddlebag before they both remount. The horses lurch up the dune and then slide down the seaward slope on their haunches to the sand flats of the foreshore.

Powdered sand whirls in the horses' footfalls as they wheel right and gallop northwards. The Indian's shouts are whipped away as he waves his hat, and I see the young bloke grit his teeth, head down, his scarlet scarf flying and his screwed-up eyes streaming in the wind's blast.

When they reach the first scatter of houses a kilometre along the beach, they dismount and lead the blowing horses over the embankment to tether them at another tavern there.

Then I shake my head as the young bloke pays a man who leads them to a dozen sandyachts behind the tavern standing ready for hire.

Sandyachts!

Similar to the ones for hire on the George Grey Flats beyond the Hutt River Lagoon at Lucky Bay. Just not as streamlined.

Their ropes clatter against thin pine masts that seem too tall for the bodywork. The hulls are constructed of light pine, low-slung and painted in barber's pole racing stripes of orange, white and blue. Their cushioned box-seats are low in the carts. Each wood-spoked wheel is rimmed with a wide circle of iron

The young bloke selects two yachts, then uncorks one of the bottles in his saddlebag. The beer erupts, and they both duck to catch the chocolate-coloured foam, open-mouthed and roaring with laughter as it splashes over them.

They wheel the yachts over the embankment to the beach.

The young bloke raises the sails, then shows the Indian the workings of the steering-rope controls, the front wheel bridle and the way the gaff-sail catches the wind.

I sense him telling the Indian to keep his eye on the sail's peak and adjust its shape to accelerate or tack as he follows the young bloke's tracks, steering between the soft sand beside the dunes and the quicksand at the water's edge fifty metres away.

The young bloke takes off and the Indian keeps the ties loose as the canvas whips and cracks and the yacht doesn't move. He settles into the seat and then hauls in the rope tied to the sail's boom. He winds it around the side cleat as the canvas fills and the yacht edges slowly forwards.

Then it cants away from the wind as he steers it towards the sand swirling in the young bloke's wake. The bellying sail opens up to the wind's full thrust, and he accelerates away.

When he slides to the floor to rest his head on the seat, the wind rips off his hat. His free hand reacts sharply, but not quick enough to save it. It cartwheels along the sand in his wake before it settles.

From that angle the sand flashes past, the craft swerving as he fights to bring the front wheels back towards the hissing edges of incoming waves. The sail lifts him in the opposite direction. He feels the play in the wheels and the tug in the sail rope, the spinning off-side wheel spokes stinging him with jets of sand as they bite and lift, bite again and rear to bite once more.

I sense the screech of spinning metal on sand, the wind's roar and the surge of shallow breakers sweeping up towards him and sliding away.

I feel the thrill run through him like ice on fire.

I hear him yell.

He has speed at his fingertips, each switch in direction and each swerve in the sail's knife-edge giving the craft more power.

I see him look up and seem to share his view as each kick of the gaff boom sways against the blue expanse of sky.

We are soaring on effortless wings.

When we look back the sand is a blurred glass carpet on which we're airborne.

We're spinning through the immensity of space, hurtling into a void.

Then we see the black wooden piles of the groyne at the end of the beach less than forty metres away. He releases the sail so that the craft cants sideways and swerves to a stop at the sea's edge beside the young bloke who's sitting on the coaming of his yacht.

Tears are streaming down the Indian's face. They look at first like the effects of the wind, but it becomes clear he's unable to control them.

His wet shirt is open, the last tie connected at his waist, and I am shocked.

I see the healing welts of horizontal scars ridged down his chest from neck to navel.

He disengages the last of the ties on his shirt, opens it wide and runs the fingers of his right hand down his chest.

For the first time in any dream that I can recall, I clearly hear him speak.

"These are my scars," he says, wiping his cheeks with the back of his left hand, "the day I lost my brother Vesak. I couldn't save him."

Vesak!

A name!

At last!

He says no more as they manoeuvre the yachts around to tack back up the beach.

To rescue his hat and start the next run downwind.

That's when I wake, my mind clear and the images still vivid as I reach over to my side table and write them down.

You want to know my first thoughts as I record the Indian's words? *The deeper scars are in his mind. I know he's grieving, but he's responding with guilt and remorse to an incident in which blame played no part.*

I wish for a moment I could have told him that. He wasn't responsible. It was an unfortunate coincidence, an accident. He did everything in his power to save his brother.

When I describe the dream to Mum and Dad, as I expected, "That has to be the Sandgroper Land Yachts down on the George Grey Flats," Dad says. "They set up business there six months ago, didn't they? What else could it mean?"

"I think it's more than that, Dad. That's the second time I've seen the Indian. I heard him speak."

"You heard him *speak* this time? Give us a break, Sonny. You, talking to the dead? He'll be introducing himself to you next. We'll have to get Doc Williams to give you an MRI or PET scan soon."

I turn off.

I leave it at that.

I excuse myself, go back to my bedroom and re-read my notes in case I have more to record for Uncle Lennard.

Chapter 7

WITHIN A MONTH, WILLIE Mack had researched self-tattooing and come up with the goods. He called us into his bedroom in Matthew Flinders House after dinner one evening to watch a youtube demo on his PC.

"It shows a young bloke self-tattooing the stencil of a severed finger with a wedding ring on it," Willie Mack explains, "on his upper thigh."

Before he fired up the video, he handed us each a single sheet on which he'd recorded the minutes of our first meeting.

The Hexagoon Flyer I read in the banner. *Number One.*

Goon, I thought. *Nice touch. But Tiny's not here tonight. I reckon he'll have something to say about a title that appears to be taking the piss. My money says he'll have us vote on that extra 'o' and it won't appear again."*

As it turned out I was right.

Willie had listed everything we'd discussed that night, right down to Tiny's mention of the Rocky Ridge Draught and the menu Mozzie had cooked up on the barbecue. He'd added a new concluding minute for a jokes' session he suggested we should have to end each meeting.

'*To lighten up the atmosphere,*' was the way he put it in the print.

Typical Willie Mack.

The first item on the agenda was Bones's fart.

> *Bruh Bones, our athlete second to none, threw caution to the wind and opened the proceedings by playing his version of our National Anthem on his double bass backside didgeridoo. It was a moment to remember, a real gas.*

And for his concluding minute he'd added a joke:

As I pointed out, Tiny was missing. He was working that weekend at the Cabinet Makers.

Anyway, the young bloke in the video was using a battery-operated needle machine.

Wearing blue surgical gloves, he cleaned and shaved the area of skin he was going to tattoo before transferring the stencil from the paper. Then, with a wet wipe in his left hand, he worked the needle over the purple lines of the severed finger design, turning them black and smearing the surplus ink across the skin to clear it for the next run. It took him no time flat by my count. Seven minutes. Even the yellow shading of the wedding ring and the blacks and greys of the finger.

It looked insane.

He made it look easy.

And even though he complained about the pain throughout the video, there was no blood. Except as part of the tattoo at the end of the severed finger. In three bright red squirting drops.

Just none of the real stuff while he was working at it.

I could see all of us thinking that was encouraging.

"So, bruhs," Willie Mack said, "all we need's the kit. I've looked into that. I reckon Dragonhawk's the one we should go for, to be honest. That'll sting us between two and three hundred bucks the lot. Inks and all. That's a fifty at the most for each of us. The needle lasts three hours and it's rechargeable so it should suit us nicely."

"We can sell it on e-bay when the job's done," Spanner broke in.

Spanner was always out to save dough. Got it from his parents, Willie Mack reckoned. "They must be descended from an O'Toole mob who starved during the potato famine in Tipperary."

Now they were alternatives, living the hippy lifestyle. They had a mud-brick house they built themselves, close to the beach in Port Gregory where Spanner's dad, Cormac, had a studio and painted seascapes, while his mother was a photographer. They hit the big time when they held a joint exhibition, but that only happened once every two years or so, which meant they were skint for most of the time in between.

Spanner had inherited their artistic skills and developed his mechanical expertise himself. He was a natural. Fix anything, given the parts. He used to make a buck on the side some weekends at the nearby Garnet Mine as a TA, when they needed a fitter's offsider.

He was an only child, and I think his takings at the time often kept the family going, even though he never talked about it. He didn't want to let the image of his parents as down-and-outers become the talk of the town.

I liked his parents, though.

Especially his father. A lot.

They were very Irish, musical and patriotic. And humorous. The story goes that Cormac O'Toole was banned for life from the Dongara Hotel when he was high on pot and made a shamrock on Paddy's Day in 2017 from a piece of green felt he cut from their pool table. Swore he hadn't done it, once he'd burned the evidence the following day. They could never prove it, according to him. "That's my story and I'm sticking to it," he said, when he told us about it.

We were often at Spanner's place when we were sliding on our cardboard packing case sleds down the dunes beside the

Hutt River where it met the Pink Lagoon. Sometimes ending up in the river when it was in flood, to cool down.

Me, I liked going to Spanner's place, especially for the tattered Art Books there and to watch Cormac—"Call me Cormac, Summer. Never mind the formalities,"—when he was in his studio painting with acrylics.

Then he started giving me lessons.

It happened like this.

The Art Books taught me about Monet, Cezanne, Mondrian, Kandinsky and especially Gauguin. Gauguin! When I saw a coloured illustration of his painting: *Where do we come from? What are we? Where are we going?* I was so dumbstruck I sat drinking it in for a full twenty minutes, before being blown away by all his other paintings.

They were truly lit!

When I showed Cormac some of my own pastels for the first time a year ago, he looked carefully through them and then said, "You have the makings, Summer. You have a gift. There's no doubt about it. You're a colourist. Another Rothko. You can't stop now. You're a natural."

I felt myself burning up, on the verge of crying.

He was working on a painting called *Man in a Pink Shirt* at the time and he'd stopped to brew a coffee. "I'll help you develop the right techniques if you'll let me. You'll never be an artist without them," he went on. "Think about it. We can fix the times."

Then he turned back to his canvas.

It showed a wrecked white yacht in the Abrolhos, the *Zero,* and a man in a pink shirt stashing a billion dollars' worth of drugs in sports bags on Burton Island under a mass of seaweed, with a sea lion closely observing him.

It was a classic.

But back to the tatts video.

"What can go wrong?" Mozzie asked. "Can it get infected?"

"You getting cold feet already?" Bones asked.

"No. I've heard stuff about kids who use a sewing needle to poke in the ink and end up in hospital," Mozzie said. "That's all."

"We'll take care," I suggested. "Medical gloves, antiseptic Dettol, the sort of wipes they use in hospitals. My Mum can get us some when she's on duty."

Willie Mack looked across at me and grinned.

I knew where that was coming from.

It was a standing joke between us.

He'd once said, imitating my Mum, ""I am the Head Nurse in this hospital, sir," Mrs Dartson told the cranky old patient with the swollen nuts. "The *Head* Nurse?" he asked. "What about the *rest* of me frickin' body? What about me testicles?" "Oh, that's easy," she replied. "You cough, and I'll check out your bouncing balls.""

Then he turned back to Mozzie. "Don't panic. We'll make sure everything's hyper hygienic. We'll get us some get some fake skin to practise on. We'll make sure we know what we're doing before we get down to the real thing."

"Sounds good to me," Bones said. Then he thought for a moment. "You said 'we'. So more than one of us is gunna be tattooing the rest of us?"

"At least two of us. One to do the other five. The second one to fix him up at the end."

"That makes sense," Bones said. "How do we choose the two?"

"We're getting ahead of ourselves," Willie Mack said, "but maybe we all give it a crack. On fake skin. Till we know what we're doing. Then we'll know who the best two are."

In February we selected Spanner and Bones to be our official tattooists. Spanner was the principal. He was the one with the steadiest hands. Bones was a close second and his assistant.

By early March we'd all been branded.

On the right hip, in the skin on the muscle above the bone.

Lying sideways on a pillow across the Hexagonal Table, we bore our right hip and half a bum cheek to Spanner.

He was really careful. A perfectionist. No rawdogging. Even with the shading.

Blue for me. Green for Mozzie. Red for Tiny and Bones. Gold for Spanner and, "What colour would you like, Willie Mack?" Spanner asked. "Green and gold, mate." Willie Mack replied. "What else! I'm true blue. I'm a ridgy-didge fair dinkum my oath g'day mate fricking Aussie!"

We all laughed at that, and none of us cried when we were having the tatts, although a couple came close. I hate to admit it, and I won't to anyone else, but I won't lie. One of them was me. It stung like I'd fallen in a nest of wasps. Brought a lump to my throat, and that wasn't my recently formed Adam's apple.

The placement was Tiny's idea.

"It's the best place for it," he said when we were discussing it in the Lyons Den. "Anywhere else'll be too obvious. Too difficult to hide. Inside the ankles is for the girls, too pussy if you ask me. The right shoulder's the obvious place but try hiding that."

"Why hide it at all," Bones asked. The shoulder had been his suggestion. "We can wear it proudly there. And once it's done, what can anyone else do about it?"

"Pride doesn't come into it, Bones. We're not doing this to put on a show. That's not what it's about. This is about us carrying out our agreed initiation ceremony. We know its meaning. We're taking a big step towards achieving what we're looking for, and keeping it to ourselves. On the hip and it's out of sight, except when we're swimming in the nud."

"Or wearing boardies in the swimming pool. That's almost in the nud, isn't it? They won't cover it." Bones argued.

"They will if you keep them up. I'm talking ninety nine percent of the time. So you and Spanner won't have to face the magistrates for giving a tattoo to someone under sixteen without a doctor's say so. You'll avoid the six months' community service or the month in the Greenough lockup, where you can't bend over in the showers if you drop the soap."

That quietened Bones down quick smart.

"Now we know exactly what to say to Rosemary Samuels, the one with the boobs to die for," Willie Mack broke in.

"What's that?" I asked.

"Tit for tat. I'll show you my tatts if you'll show me your tits."

That started the-end-of-meeting joke session, during which we'd agreed one of us was allowed to tell a joke they'd dreamed up.

This time it was Spanner's turn.

"Talking of boobs, what were the five queens doing when they were sprinting flat out down Oxford Street all sequined up in their wigs and high heels, their mascara running down their cheeks with the sweat?" he asked.

"I don't know," Mozzie said, "What?"

"Having a drag race."

'One blue bean," Tiny said when the laughter died down, and I delivered it.

"And now, us bruhs of the Hexagonal Table," Tiny went on, "we need to get our heads together and dream up a challenging quest."

Dream up? I thought. *Dream up! I know exactly what we have to do.*

Chapter 8

IN MARCH, 2024, I had my most vivid dream yet.

Never mind the snake pit, the shark attack or the sandyachts. This time I was caught up in a raging storm.

It may have had to do with the lessons we'd had that day at the Windsurfing Club on Coronation Beach, north of Geraldton. It was an all-day school excursion and one of our optional sports.

The area is famous for its winds. Even the trees bow down to them and grow parallel to the ground. The latest three-day Wave Rally windsurfing World Championships was held there last week. We watched it on TV, and it was breathtaking.

Anyway, the wind that day we went was a howling gale and the chop ferocious.

It was insane, muscle-tearing fun. Airborne dizzily one minute, juddering across the chop the next with your teeth clattering in your skull, capsized the moment after that.

Try righting yourself in those conditions!

When you're fourteen.

Beats lifting weights.

In this particular dream I found myself in Cape Town. I recognised Table Mountain and the Lion's Head. You can't mistake them. I've often watched the Aussies play test cricket against the Proteas on TV at the Newlands ground, with the Lion's Head rearing up behind it.

So there I was, hovering over the harbour, looking down at the sailing ships.

There was a fleet of twenty or so three-masters and smaller vessels anchored in the bay.

I saw that two of them were preparing to set sail.

One was my ghost ship, the other a smaller ship of a different design.

If you're wondering how I recognised my ghost ship from above, I can't explain. I was simply drawn to it, forced in some weird way to concentrate on it.

The anchors were part way up, their ropes hanging vertically as they approached the surface trailing clouds of mud. I could see the wide wooden anchor stocks ten metres down as they rose.

The ship was drifting slowly backwards, on the current or the wind.

One mainsail was set part way, the canvas backing on the mast.

That's when I landed on the deck and got a ringside view.

As usual, no one took any notice of me.

The first thing that astonished me was the black-headed sheep. Or were they goats? More than thirty of them were tightly packed together in a pen against the rails, panting. A few with their tongues hanging out. And a big mob of cackling light brown chickens beside them, with their nesting boxes under netting.

Then I watched five sailors manning the capstan on the port side—that's the left if you're not certain. They were winding in a circular line attached to the main anchor rope, another crew of sailors sprinting round the line, tying it to the anchor rope and untying it turn and turnabout as the line wound up the capstan, and the anchor rope came in.

The tension in the anchor rope sprayed seawater across the slippery decks as it disappeared down to the deck below, where I assumed other sailors were coiling it for storage.

That's when I saw him.

The Indian!

Right beside me, and I hadn't noticed him!

He had a bucket in both hands and was hurling sand across the deck, I assumed to control the slipperiness for the sprinters with the ties bringing in the anchor rope.

A shock of recognition burned through me like an oxy flame.

I've rarely felt such excited familiarity before.

It was late evening, and the Indian had disappeared into his cabin behind the bow when the ships, with their anchors bound to the rails, set further sails, picked up the wind and gathered speed.

The sun was setting as we—I say we because I was still aboard—glided past Robben Island into the open sea, where the black Atlantic met the deep blue of the Indian Ocean.

We disappeared into the darkness, surging onto the rolling swells, riding diagonally up one side and plunging directly down the other as if that's what the ships were built for.

When the sun rose the next morning, the smaller ship was several kilometres behind.

My ghost ship had swung south, where the winds were strong and fresh. She entered the menacing blue-black Southern-Ocean, now a series of rolling, hollowed waves, overtaking her and lined with flying foam.

She was under full sail now, with extra sails on each side attached to poles stretching way out beyond her beam. Their ends almost caught the wave-crests as she swayed from one beam to the other, surging and settling and lifting to ride successive swells. She was flying, accelerating down the backs of waves she flung aside as she sighed up the next, stinging wind-spray sweeping down the decks.

Wow! It took my breath away. That's the simplest way I can express the feeling of elation.

By mid-afternoon the second day, the smaller ship had disappeared below the horizon behind us.

Fast forward three weeks.

Rising right beside us, we looked at the rocky cliffs and saw the knee-high waving grasses on the slopes of Amsterdam Island and the inviting half-circle of the volcanic lagoon of its neighbor, St Paul Island.

That's when we altered course north-eastwards on a long diagonal sweep into the wide and welcoming Indian Ocean.

For five weeks the weather held.

We plunged on across a vast expanse of boisterous sunlit seas. The broad, dark clouds of towering storm-fronts we saw to the south, distantly menacing and split with sudden lightning, threatened to sweep up towards us but did not reach our latitude, though we sometimes felt the icy bite in the winds.

On an east-north-east bearing, we sailed away from an ocean of storms towards the welcoming tropics and the sun.

I often saw the Indian, and believe it or not, the young bloke who took him sandyachting, working among the crew or relaxing on the deck when they were off duty.

The Indian sometimes played a red squeezebox. He was learning it, and picking it up remarkably fast, the parakeet raising its neck feathers as though it disapproved of its squawky notes when he had it perched on his shoulder. I'd watched him bid for it, when one of the sailors died three days out from Cape Town. His belongings were auctioned off, after the corpse wrapped in canvas with a cannon ball for company slid down the chute into the sea.

For some weeks I watched him carve two pieces of what looked like ebony into a pair of goggles, similar to those he wore during the shark attack. They looked like shiny black serviette rings similar to Mum's when he'd finished. It took him a week to shape the lenses from a pane of glass, grinding them with great care and concentration on a whetstone similar to the one we use in the Lyons Den to sharpen fishhooks, and then glue them to the ebony.

I had to laugh when he eventually tested each lens.

He filled his hat with seawater and stuck his face into it, first holding the lens over his left eye, then the right. Each time he came up grinning, all white teeth, as he had been when diving for coins. Once when he did it, the parakeet went nuts, flying the length of its drawstring and flapping its frantic wings like it was headed for Sri Lanka—if that's where the Indian was from.

I sometimes overheard the officers discuss their sailing instructions as we progressed. While I couldn't clearly understand their pig gibberish, the more I heard it I sort of got a clue.

Enough to guess the rest.

When we reached the 27th parallel of latitude, I understood, we'd sight our target for the first time—the north-western coast of Nieuw Holland. That landfall would be a signal to change course. We'd sail north along the continent, before turning north-west across the Timor Sea towards the Sunda Straits and our destination port of Batavia in Java.

You mean we'll make a landfall north of Geraldton? I wondered, when I overheard them discuss it the first time. They were concerned about the uncertainty with which they measured longitude. *We'll reach the right latitude, that's for certain, but if they're unsure of their longitude how close will we be to the coast? Will we bypass the maze of reefs of the Abrolhos Islands in time to miss them? Talk about the* Titanic! *We don't want to end up like the* Batavia, *wrecked near Beacon Island in 1629.*

Each day I watched an officer slot the black and white metal letters and numbers into the calendar above the ship's public watch roster, like he was altering the details on a cricket scoreboard.

The latest date was Donderdag, 2 Juni, 1712.

Donderdag? Thursday, maybe. June for sure.

For the first day in weeks, we faced the black front of a threatening storm streaming up from the south, sweeping in towards the hidden continent.

There were still no signs of land—no birds, no whales, no inshore tell-tale streaks of weed or red-brown lines of coral spawn edging the current from horizon to horizon.

We watched the dark lines of cloud stretch across the bluest sky, threatening to shut out the sun and bringing us the first cold gusts of a wind shift that unsettled the run of waves we'd been surfing across.

The swirling seas lifted during the morning to surge and hiss across our beam.

Stinging spray drove across the midship deck.

I should know. I felt it. I was soaked and freezing.

The sea was eerily lit in foaming patches of fluorescent green as the sun streamed through the last breaks in the cloud before the lashing rain closed in. The winds gusted to a roar and the blue of the horizon greyed to black as the sailors worked to prepare the ship before she felt the full force of the gale.

It was a hectic time for them.

Below decks I watched them remove the snouts of the cannons from the portholes. They were dragged on the wooden wheels of their carriages alongside ship's inner planking. There they were lashed tight to hooks in the beams and their wheels were chocked. Then the portholes were locked down

The young bloke and the Indian among others worked in the howling wind to cover the hatch-gratings with protective canvas battened down to the decks. They did the same to the passageway entrances, leaving a canvas flap to allow a single crewman entry at a time.

The ropes were disconnected from the bow anchors and stored below.

That worried me.

It means we can't use the anchors in an emergency. I thought. *What if we want to slam on the brakes in an emergency? Have they thought of that?*

At one point I followed the young bloke and the Indian below decks to the very bottom of the ship.

I couldn't believe what I saw.

There were triangular wedges chocked into the base of the three masts, and the Indian, instructed by the young bloke, sledge-hammered them firmly back into place. They had already loosened as the masts shifted under the growing power of the wind.

What? Is he gunna have to do that during the storm? I wondered. *Rather him than me. What if a mast comes down? I'm not wearing a hard hat.*

Back on deck, the ship's three boats were covered in canvas and lashed tight around the main mast. Safety lines were run from stern to bow along the decks, now soaked and slippery as bathroom tiles, and one of the officers organised a knotted line to hang from the stern, in case anyone was swept overboard.

Good thinking, I thought, *I'm already fighting to keep my balance.*

The skipper and the officers decided to scud before the wind with the storm sails set, with lines round the sails to save them from ballooning out and ripping in the raging wind. It took them two hours for the change, but the ship immediately responded. She ran before the wind, holding her course and balancing as the new set of sails lifted the bows and deepened the stern.

The frightening shuddering in the ship's frame eased.

It seemed their decision was the right one.

The alternative, I understood, was to remove the sails altogether and sail with the masts bare and a sea anchor, like an airport windsock, towed behind to hold the course. To do that in these rising seas we risked being swept broadside on and swamped by the waves or being flung sideways on a surge that could tear away the rudder and capsize us.

No thanks, I thought. *Stick with your first decision.*

By evening the preparations were complete and the ship was in the wild grip of the storm.

She was driven by screaming winds on a north-east bearing, ploughing into deeply hollow seas that burst across her bows.

The spray was flung high across the foremast sail. Caught in the wind, it gusted across the mid-ship deck and the navigation bridge, blinding the officers clinging to the rail there even though they had the shelter of a canvas awning.

Two sailors were bent double, bracing themselves at the steering whip staff—we didn't have a wheel, but a long pole that moved from port to starboard attached to the rudder's tiller to steer the ship. They fought to control the unfamiliar swaying of the ship, struggling to keep the wind coming at them from the south, or the ship would swing sideways and capsize.

I guess they were thankful they weren't able to see the terrifying following waves climbing mast high behind her and roaring past as she surged up, then raced down their slopes.

I couldn't bear to look back either.

I was shitting myself, to be honest.

As usual, in a situation like this.

The lookout seated up in the crow's nest swinging across the sky had lashed himself to the fore mast. He was peering above the wind-flung spray, shielding his eyes as best he could, but blinded by the driving rain. Now and then I heard him singing as if he was enjoying the show, his songs intermittently drowned out by the wind's roar and the shriek of the rigging.

For one weird hour on dusk the rain turned into a thunderous downpour of hail.

The golf-ball sized stinging chunks scattered across the blackened decks, turning them into rippled ice as successive waves of spray washed over them and the last of the light faded.

That evening most of the crew were below, sitting out the storm.

The deck below was stifling when I went to take a look, the smoky stench of swinging whale-oil lamps choking. When I looked in, thirty or so sailors on the next watch were waiting for the ship's bell to ring to end the previous watch. That would be their signal to take to the decks for the next four hours to midnight.

I could smell the gin on their breath—or was it rum? Either way it was for Dutch courage. Not one of them was smiling. I saw a look of resignation on most of their expressions, or what I took for resignation through the grey smoke of the thin-stemmed white clay pipes they were choofing on.

So that's the vape of the early eighteenth century, I remember thinking.

Moments before the bell, I went to the forward deck beneath the bow.

I knew that the Indian and the young bloke had cabins there.

I'd followed them there many times during the voyage, to check them out.

The young bloke, who I gathered from what I'd witnessed was the senior carpenter on board, had a cabin to himself. It was on the port side, with a cannon in it, the black snout of its barrel usually pointing out through the porthole. Now it was lashed sideways to the hooks on the inner planks, and the porthole was closed.

The Indian shared his cabin on the other side of the passageway with another carpenter. He had the top bunk. The cabin doubled as the carpenter's storeroom, with spare timbers and all their tools lashed from floor to ceiling beside them.

When I got there, the young bloke had left the others in the carpenter's store.

He'd closed their cabin door, so we could no longer hear the sounds of the Indian's red squeezebox as he stepped into his cabin.

As he did so, the ship heeled wildly to port, echoing to the booming roar of timber screeching across rock.

He was flung violently across the cabin and hurled to the floor.

He couldn't protect himself from the cannon as the floor tilted wildly back towards him and the rear of the cannon carriage tore free from its lashings.

It swung outwards as the ship canted almost vertically, wrenching the oak wheel of the gun-carriage in a half-circle across the cabin.

It crashed into his right leg, snapping the bone above the ankle as he was thrown back towards the door swinging on its hinges behind him.

I saw him react to the shock and searing pain as he knew with sickening horror that he'd been seriously injured. He fought to swing his legs out of the way as the ship righted herself and the cannon rolled back towards the paneling.

Then she pitched violently over in the direction she'd been sailing and the thunder of tearing timbers echoed through her frame.

The young bloke slid in agony across the tilting floor away from the door.

I watched in shocked disbelief as the sea swirled through the fractured planking. The impact of the swinging cannon had ruptured the panels and the outer timbers of the hull, and though the beams were holding, the water foamed through the split timbers as the waves crashed over them.

I knew at that distorted angle that his cabin was submerged, and I sensed his terror at his helplessness.

He was about to drown.

Another thunderous roar echoed through the ship as she slewed across rocks that tore into her holds, the explosion of smashing timbers subsiding to a series of unearthly groans as the bows skidded and then held. The stern swung wildly with the wind and seas as she screeched sideways, explosive cracks deafening as the rudder tore away.

Mountainous waves crashed over her as she lay on her side, lifting her and grinding her across the shelf of rock.

Her sails on shuddering masts were filled with wind and water, as if they were still driving her towards the horizon she would never reach.

On the decks I saw a mess of twisted rigging and smashed masts.

The navigation deck was empty except for the carcasses of two black-headed sheep drowned and swept into a corner.

The officers must have been flung overboard when she struck, their chart table wrenched from its stays and hurled with their instruments into the darkness.

Some of the crew on watch who had survived the first impact were clinging to the rigging and the safety lines, their shouting shadows struggling towards the relative safety of the stern as the raging seas swirled over them.

In the foremast crow's nest the lookout hung limp, bent double. The ropes that had lashed him to the mast must have snapped his spine when the ship struck, cutting short his scream of warning as the towering cliffs loomed through the rain at the last moment.

Now I could see them, less than fifty metres dead ahead, the roar of crashing breakers thundering below them as the foam rushed part way up the cliffs and back.

I was terrified and fought to wake up.

Once again, I struggled to regain consciousness.

It felt like I was suffocating in a vacuum without oxygen as

I gasped for breath. And then, when I could bear it no longer, I burst awake, flooded with relief.

My ghost ship was wrecked, but I was back in my familiar world.

My heart was hammering at my throat.

It took me several minutes to calm myself.

The images were so sharp and vivid it was like I was still connected to the dream, and I couldn't help wondering, *What happened to the young bloke? Did he survive? If so, what happened next?*

I decided to risk it and mention it to Mum.

Dad was thankfully up at Denham attending a meeting of the Senior Malgana Men.

Of course, she mentioned the *Batavia* at first. 1629. She thought it had to be the prediction—if you can call it that—of something in the past.

Then she thought about it and suggested an interpretation that made sense to me for the first time.

"What about the *Zuytdorp*?" she asked. "You said the date on board was 1712, didn't you. Wasn't she wrecked that year? I think you're onto something this time, Suma, with another prediction of the past. Ask Uncle Lennard. He will know, for sure. He might even get his novel out to check."

"I'll do that."

I didn't mention the exercise book notes I was writing for him. Or my telephone calls. I kept them to myself.

Until the next meeting of the six Alpha Bruhs of the Hexagonal Table, when I brought it up.

Chapter 9

Ｉ FOUND THE BOOK *Carpet Of Silver* in the school library. Uncle Lennard had told me it was about the wreck's discovery and the investigation that followed, and I found it so interesting I couldn't put it down. I read it in two days, and then had a second read, taking notes.

According to the evidence, there were survivors.

The Indian and the young bloke may have been among them!

Except for the poor bloke in the crow's nest. He died for sure, if my dream was accurate. *Maybe they had to eat him*, the awful thought crossed my mind before I could drive it away.

"Fingers and toes crossed," Mum said when I told her. "Maybe the young carpenter didn't drown after all, and he and the Indian were among the others who made it to the cliff top."

"I hope so," I said. "That can't be the last of my dreams with them in it."

What about the young bloke's smashed ankle? How did it heal? I wondered.

Who knows?

I don't.

Yet.

One thing was for sure and certain, to be honest. I had to get to the wreck site and see it for myself.

"I've got an idea about a quest," I told the bruhs at our next meeting in the Lyons Den.

"What's that," Tiny asked.

"Well, I haven't told you guys, but I've been having these dreams. Weird ones. Don't think I'm delulu if I tell you they're about the *Zuytdorp* when she was wrecked. I've been aboard and getting to know a couple of the crew. Specially this Indian kid. I've dreamed about him several times."

"One of them's an *Indian*? On a sailing ship three hundred years ago? And he's your mate now?" Bones asked. He held out his right forefinger. "Pull this."

There's no way I was gunna do that, especially not with Bones. If you take the risk, he sounds like a fully inflated balloon when you let the air out, squeezing the mouthpiece together. He can shoot a blue flame brighter than a welder's, so we have to wear shades.

"No cap, Bones. It's true," I said, then hesitated, unsure whether to go on, but before I could stop them the words came out of my mouth as if they were travelling faster than sound. "I've even thought his thoughts. Been in a snake pit with him. Survived a shark attack. Sailed a sandyacht three hundred years ago. Played a red squeezebox that belonged to a dead bloke. Carved a piece of ebony."

"Carved a piece of ebony? What is he now? A *carpenter*?" Tiny asked. "Sheesh! So that's where you are when you're missing in action, you poor bugger. Off with the fairies."

It's true.

With colours anyway.

There are times when I see something so colourful I can't take my eyes off it. For as long as it takes. The burnt orange and brilliant yellows in the marigolds in Mum's veggie patch. The changing shades of blue in a winter sky. Bushfire flames. You name it, I'm in there mixing my pastels like you wouldn't believe, as if nothing else matters.

But they weren't taking me seriously.

I started feeling cranky.

"Say what you like, my dreams are so real it's like I'm there. I'm the one having them, not you," I said.

"Take it easy, Summer. Don't spit the dummy and fall off your high horse, you might break your neck," Willie Mack said. "They're not taking the piss. It's hard to believe, is all, and they're expressing that, as all us Aussies do. It's part of our nature. You taught me that. Tell us more."

I calmed down. Willie Mack always had that effect on me when it counted.

Then I told them about the storm and the shipwreck. In full detail. And they listened without comment for once.

"That was some story," Mozzie said when I'd finished. "You should write it and send it to a magazine."

"Yeah, *Playboy*," Bones said drily, as if he was still dissing me. "My dad says they're publishing it again as an annual in 2025. Your Indian might even get to be the centerfold if he's game to take his kurta pajama off."

"His kurta pajama? What's that?" Spanner asked.

"A swanky dress for Indian men," Bones replied. "The sort of gear you wouldn't be seen dead in."

"Okay, enough! Gloves on!" I shouted and stormed out to the ring.

Bones followed me, and when I reached for the gloves, he put his left arm around my shoulder and held out his right hand. "Stay cool, bruh," he said. "No need for a showdown. You know me."

"Yeah, we know you, shit for brains," Willie Mack said. He'd followed us out to referee. "A good crap would take a load off your mind."

"What, the two of you now?" Bones said. "I'm sorry, Summer. It comes out sometimes, before I can stop it. I've got to learn to think first."

"Yeah, empathy. With you that's as likely as a barking hotdog, Bones."

"I'll get there."

"You'd better."

I looked down at Bones's hand, hesitated, then shook it and followed the two of them back inside.

"Better now?" Tiny asked, choofing on his vape. "So what's the quest, bruh?"

Before I began, the thought crossed my mind, *Bones. He's a runner. That's why he's so aggressive. He has to win. Feel any empathy for the opposition and you're relegating yourself to second place before you hit the tape. He's alright, if you look at it that way. I've got to learn to put up with him. Can't have him lose his next race because I've got a thin skin. He's so promising an athlete. That's his gift to the world. He's another Herb Elliott. Hasn't lost an 800 or 1500 metre race for his age group yet.*

Then I explained—and the bruhs all agreed.

The *Zuytdorp* wreck site!

Here we come! The six Alpha Bruhs of the Hexagonal Table!

It took us four weeks' preparation—to make three long distance phone calls to the Shipwrecks' Museum in Perth, to visit the Museum of Geraldton, to contact Murchison House Station and to convince my dad to talk the Department of Environment and Conservation in Shark Bay into giving us permission to visit the wreck site, which was a prohibited area.

With a weekend free during the April vacation in 2024, we set off in Tiny's Jeep Wrangler, waving four hard won permits.

We went through Murchison House Station from Kalbarri, rather than taking the track from the Northwest Coastal Highway down the vermin fence, or the other track from Shark Bay through Tamala Station. We heard the fence-line track hadn't been graded and was overgrown; and Tamala Station was refusing visitors to avoid the spread of poisonous weeds.

No firearms, we were told. And no climbing down the cliff faces to avoid erosion.

Too easy. No probs.

Tiny would leave his .22 Ruger bolt-action Dugite repellent at home, and we'd look for a place we could dive straight into the sea from the clifftops without touching the slopes, with a knotted rope—like the one I dreamed hanging off the stern of the *Zuytdorp*—to climb back up.

The only bruh who cringed at the idea of the high dive and the climb was Mozzie, and we all understood why. Both his phobias in one hit were too much for him.

"Not me," he said. "I'll give it a miss."

"Wait till we get there," Tiny said. "You never know, it may not be as bad as it looks. We'll help you handle it."

"By leaving me alone and not doing it at all," Mozzie insisted.

Bones put his arm across his shoulder. "Don't back off till you know what you're facing, bruh," he said. "Imagine it's another fricking opponent in the ring and you're about to beat the living shit out of him. Like you always do."

"Win on points, you mean."

"Exactly. Make a point of winning."

We took off first thing Friday morning, towing Tiny's stepfather's trailer loaded with jerry cans of fuel and water, our camping, diving and fishing gear, the knotted rope, a shovel and a toilet roll.

Me, I brought along a sketch pad and my pastels in a grey celluloid Philip Morris cigar box Aunty Alicia gave me. "This belonged to my papá when he was a boy," she told me. "He kept his rock collection in it. I know you'll take good care of it."

Spanner brought one of his mum's cameras, a battered Nikon FA.

We called in to Murchison House Station to thank them for their permit and get their advice about the tracks.

"Go north the long way inland if you want to get there quickly," one of the backpacker station hands told us. He was a good-natured, pony-tailed Belgian with a thick accent. "I took that way two weeks ago, shooting vermin goats. It's not too rough and fairly clear. When you get to the fence, head for the coast. You can't miss it."

"If we do, we're in the ocean and heading for Africa and Europe," Willie Mack laughed. "Give us your address and we'll call in and see your folks back in Brussels—to tell them you haven't been bitten by the red-back on the toilet seat."

"*Yet*," Tiny broke in.

"In Ghent, actually," the Belgian corrected him. "No chance with the red-back. We have a can of Mortein in there all the time. For the blowies mostly."

"Good thinking, so do we," Tiny said.

"And good luck with the drive. You should have no problems."

We crossed the Murchison River, and it was running. Just. There must have been some rain up in the Gascoyne catchment, but not much.

We took the Belgian's advice, ignoring the enticing tracks leading off to the left and avoiding the deep gullies running inland from the cliffs, eroded by rainfall runoff over centuries.

The Banksias were in full bloom, their vertical orange and yellow flowers flashing like amber warning lamps in their crinkly olive foliage. There were hundreds of them, thriving in the semi-desert rocky, sandy landscape.

I loved their glowing colours.

Couldn't get enough.

Was off with the fairies again.

Until we reached the fence, turned left, ploughed through a belt of overgrown Ti trees, ducking to avoid the whipping branches, and arrived at the wreck site.

It was a revelation.

It was like coming home, to the lowest point along the towering cliffs, an easy three-stage climb down to the breakers at their foot.

It looks as if Coincidence took pity on the survivors, I thought, when I leapt out, sprinted to the edge and looked down. *This is the only place for kilometres where they could make it to the cliff top. Anywhere else and they were dead meat.*

The wind was up, the tide was in, and the little blowholes were steaming spray when you least expected them to, as if they were stoked to see us and were putting on a show. Not many people visited these days. Not since the area had been declared a National Park.

So this is where the survivors lit a gigantic signal fire to attract the passing ships, I realised. To roast the dead sheep they'd scavenged from the wreck and smash the gin bottles they'd recovered, after partying like it was 1999 for the first three nights after the storm, to celebrate their survival.

That's where a sailor placed the wooden statuette ripped from the stern—the one in the glass cabinet in the Shipwrecks' Museum now—part way down the cliff, to let future generations know they'd camped there. It was painted yellow in my dream.

This is where the young senior carpenter sat in the shade for two months, leaning against a Ti tree—maybe this one here, it looks old enough—while his leg healed and the Indian brought him heated seawater to clean the splinted wound.

This is where the Indian set out from with his bucket each day, to look for fresh water collected in the gnamma-hole rainwater seepages in the gullies to the north.

And maybe, just maybe, this is where the Malgana family came across them in August 1712, during the winter rains, when they were travelling south to the Murchison River on their annual walkabout to meet their Nhanda brothers and sisters there. To share in the late run of tasty blue manna and mangrove crabs and crack an oyster or two from the intertidal rocks.

How did I dream up all that?

Vaguely, so maybe I'm wrong, but I like to think I'm right.

I have a feeling I am.

Anyway.

Mozzie was up and running the moment Tiny parked, fossicking in the scrub.

"Hey, you guys! You have to come and look at this!" he shouted minutes later. "I've found a Greater Stick Rats' nest. They're supposed to be extinct on the mainland."

He showed us a warren of nests, woven with twigs, in a patch of heath beside the Ti tree belt. A squirming bundle of seven tiny, grey-nosed pinkies was coiled together in one.

He was stoked. "These must be related to the ones they rehabilitated on Salutation Island three years ago. The *Return to 1616 Project* they called it. They must've swum or rafted across to the mainland. I can't believe it! Spanner, can I borrow your camera?"

When we left him, another shout told us he'd found a second warren.

And then another.

And later still, another.

He'd recorded twenty-one by the time we took off three days later.

I spent Saturday and part of Sunday sketching, trying my hand at seascape-landscapes in Cormac's style, to capture everything I was seeing. The wreck site and the boiling breakers where I imagined the ship's skeleton still lay. The tall cliffs each side of the wreck site. The yellow spit of sand we discovered at the base of cliffs half a kilometre to the south.

And especially the steep-sided inlet a hundred metres further on, where swirling water several metres or so below us foamed into a circular pool and thundered into grottoes beneath our feet.

Ideal for our dive.

"This is fire," Tiny said. "Better than we hoped for. Who's first? We need to test the depth. It looks okay to me."

He threw a fist-sized rock in and we followed it down, until it splashed in and was obscured by a spread of lace-like foam. When it cleared we could see it glimmering on the sandy bottom.

"Looks can be deceptive," Spanner said, "with water like this. It could be too shallow."

"I'll risk it," Bones said. "It's not that far a drop."

"No. I'm the oldest," Tiny said. "It's my responsibility. The tide looks as if it's on the turn. There's not a lot of time. Fix the rope."

Willie Mack tied the rope around a boulder at the lip and threw it over the side. It met the surface of the water and then some.

Tiny stripped to his boardies, walked to the edge, took one look down and shouting, "*Geronimo!*" he leapt off feet first, his arms to his sides, his legs stiffly together.

Geronimo? I echoed him in my mind. *My Suma Apache? That makes sense. Take a risk. No pain, no gain.*

He hit the water, sank and almost immediately reappeared, bursting through the erupting whirlpool his body had made on entry, laughing.

"Too easy," he shouted, treading water and looking up at us. "It's not that deep, so no diving in headfirst. Be prepared when you reach the bottom to push up with your feet."

He swam across to the rope and hauled himself up, knot by knot, until Spanner helped him crawl over the lip.

By the time he reached the top we were all in our boardies.

"Who's next?" he asked, as Bones took a run and wind-milled into the air, arms and legs flailing. He landed part way across the pool, resurfacing with a scream of delight, "It's freezing me bloody nuts off! They're up inside me keeping warm," as he headed for the rope.

After that it was first come, first served, sometimes two at once, once even three, hanging on together for dear life as if our hands were stuck with the araldite I mentioned before, tighter than a snake's you know what.

Us Alpha Bruhs of the Hexagonal Table.

We'd been branded.

We'd come on a quest of sorts.

We'd passed the next test.

All except for Mozzie.

We could see him in the distance, clicking away with the camera like he was David Attenborough's offsider.

Our shouts must have carried to him.

He was taking his time catching up with us, working his way slowly and reluctantly towards us across the saltbush heath.

Hoping we weren't looking for him, no doubt.

"I'll go and get him," Bones said.

"Don't frighten him off," Tiny said. "He has to do this his own way and in his own time, if he's gunna do it at all. We're his bruhs and we have to help him through it. Be reasonable with him."

"Jawohl, mein kapitän," Bones said with a Nazi salute as he took off.

"*Smartarse!*" Tiny shouted after him. "Three blue beans!"

Mozzie saw him coming. Before he could turn around and resume his photographic patrol back to the car, Bones had sprinted over and put his left arm around his shoulder

They walked slowly towards us.

When they reached us, the cold wind was starting up.

The skin on Bones's arms appeared to still have goosebumps and his palms were wrinkled.

Mozzie looked resigned.

Trapped.

He handed the camera back to Spanner.

He was wearing his boardies and a green t-shirt with a Bush Turkey printed on it with its wings spread. I knew it was one of his Nhanda totems. Worn for good luck.

He stopped ten metres from the lip of the pool, sat down and crossed his legs.

"This is as far as I come," he said.

"For now," Willie Mack said, gently. He waved a hand at the five of us and we formed a pentagonal circle around him, then sat down as he had, cross-legged, facing him.

He had his eyes closed.

He was breathing heavily.

I thought for one dreadful moment he was about to start crying.

Then what would we do?

But he didn't.

We didn't speak and neither did he.

Several long minutes later, he shuffled a metre closer, still with his eyes closed, and we adjusted our positions to maintain the circle.

It must have taken us an hour as a group to patiently get within a metre of the lip, with Mozzie opening his eyes now and then before closing them and shuffling forward. He was taking in deep breaths and blowing out the air through pursed lips, as if he was oxygenating up for the challenge of his life or a world record deep dive.

That's when Spanner had to move to avoid falling backwards into the pool. We shifted position so that he could rejoin the circle.

"Alright, Mozzie," Tiny said when he made another small shift forward. "You've aced it so far. Half a metre to go and you'll be sizing up the challenge. Remember, us bruhs are with you. You can open your eyes now."

He did and froze. We heard him choke.

From his angle he couldn't see the water's surface, just the edge of a depthless chasm with the swirling sea, lower now, hissing within it like an echo chamber. He gave out another frightened gasp when Willie Mack reached out, took both his hands and helped him stand.

Now he could see the water and take in the immensity of what he was about to do.

If he was gunna do it.

At Tiny's signal four of us jumped in to wait for him, leaving Tiny and Willie Mack to talk him through it.

He was pale and quivering as he took a fearful shuffle forward, stiffly, like someone struggling from a butcher's deep freeze after being locked in there with the frozen carcasses overnight.

Then, without a sound, he did not look down, took another involuntary step forward and was airborne.

I could see the Bush Turkey on his t-shirt flying towards us, as if coming in to land.

He hit the water at an awkward angle, but came up on his own, dog paddling to keep afloat.

He grinned at us, like Bazza barking at the seagulls or Captain Cook thinking all his Christmases had come at once.

Which in Mozzie's case they had!

He refused our help, dog-paddled to the rope and worked his way up.

And then, without another word, he measured out a ten metre run-up, spun round and took a second airborne leap at full sprint, landing beyond us as we cheered him on.

But that was it.

When he climbed out, he turned silently away and walked towards the car.

He did not look back.

I could see his shoulders shaking.

Chapter 10

UNCLE LENNARD AND AUNTY Alicia passed through Geraldton on their way to Northampton three weeks later. They stopped in the city for two nights while Aunty Alicia caught up with the Yamaji Language Centre, giving me the opportunity to meet with Uncle Lennard one on one.

I couldn't wait to see him.

We met in Skeetas Café on the waterfront beside the Museum of Geraldton and I showed him my exercise books and my sketches of the wreck site.

He took his time turning the pages of both, not commenting at first.

And then, "You have been busy, Suma," he said at last. "Frankly I'm amazed. At your diligence with the notes and your talent with the pastels. Especially with the latter. You know who your pastels remind me of?"

I felt my face burn. "Who?"

"Rover Thomas, from the East Kimberley."

"My friend Cormac O'Toole told me exactly the same thing the other day," I said breathlessly. "He thinks I'm following in the footsteps of Rover Thomas and Mark Rothko. Cormac's an artist helping me develop my techniques. He has a studio in Port Gregory."

"Well, that confirms it, then. Have you seen any of Rover's work?"

"I've googled him. I can see what you and Cormac mean."

"Well, you're applying the same blocks of colour to interpret the landscape, though his perspective is more aerial than yours, and less naïve. I can see you aiming for the same effect, though. That will come with time. I especially like your palette. Your mixes. You've got some interesting colours..." he flicked through the sketchbook, "... in this one here, especially, where you're looking down at where the wreck ended up and across the ocean to the horizon, with a minimum of sky. That's a fantastic range of blues. They're *deadly*, by crikey. Is it your favourite colour?"

"One of them. Burnt orange I like. Violet. Some others."

"Rover preferred his familiar Western Desert ochres. Brown, red, apricot, yellow and black as I recall."

He leaned both elbows on the table, linked his fingers and leaned his chin on his thumbs as the young Asian Australian waitress in her smart black uniform put his coffee and my milkshake on the table, her face lit with a smile Uncle Lennard acknowledged.

Then he gazed at me with his blue and brown eyes thoughtfully for a long minute. I saw a touch of humour and concern in his expression and felt my stomach tighten.

"I don't need to tell you you've got something going here, Suma. You've lit the flame. Now you've got to keep the fires burning. It won't be easy, but you're on the right track. The world is going to need men like you when the time comes. Men who know what it is to be men. Men who don't sit around and complain, but create, and work towards building a better world than the one they were born into."

Then he did something extraordinary.

He reached inside the neck of his navy-blue shirt and withdrew a leather thong from around his neck. It had an oval abalone shell pendant dangling on it. I'd never seen it before. When he laid it face up on the table I saw there was a seabird, an albatross or sea eagle, etched across the whirling greens and blues.

It has to be a sea eagle, I thought. *An osprey. My personal totem.*

Next, he leaned sideways to get his wallet from the pocket of his jeans. He undid the lid to the purse and took out a battered silver coin. He placed it carefully on the table beside the pendant, then pushed them both across to me as he lifted his coffee cup, took a sip and wiped his upper lip with the back of his hand.

I was hyper alert to his every move, and nervously on edge.

What's coming next? I wondered.

He tapped my dreaming exercise books. "You may not know that Rover Thomas was a psychic, too."

Too? The thought raced through my mind as he spoke. *Me a psychic like Rover Thomas?*

I had no idea what he was talking about.

I felt both alert and slightly dizzy, as if I was on the verge of passing out and yet sharply aware, as I had been in the snake pit. Was there another Gabon Viper beneath my foot? The Diamond Rattlesnake Dad had mentioned?

"He was a psychic of the Desert Dreaming, Suma. He was in touch with the consciousness of a deceased relative, and he created the ceremonial dances, songs and images that were passed on to him. He referred to them as the Krill Krill. Sacred works of great beauty and significance. Just as you've been doing here, with your pastels and the stories of the Indian and his friend."

He lifted his coffee cup and blew across its surface, cooling it before it burned his lips again. He took a sip and put it down.

"Right. Now, let's get to the heart of the matter, Suma. You're going to have to concentrate, so listen carefully, by crikey. Your Indian's name is Sunil Dewaraja. You already know his brother's name was Vesak. I know it's Sunil, because his name was added to the crew list for the *Zuytdorp*'s second journey back to Middelburg, when she was anchored in Galle Harbour in 1708."

I interrupted him. "Galle Harbour? Is that in India or Sri Lanka?"

"In Sri Lanka, but it was known as Ceylon then."

"And Middelburg?"

"That's in the Netherlands, in the south. It's in the state of Zeeland, actually, where the *Zuytdorp* was built in 1701. That's where you were, when you dreamed about the ship returning home in 1709."

I nodded, excitement running through me like electricity. It made the hair on the back of my head stand up like Spanner was jump-starting me with a pair of leads attached to the Wrangler, with Tiny revving the accelerator.

All the scrambled pieces of the puzzling jigsaw were falling into place.

Sunil Dewaraja!

G'day, bruh. I thought. *It's good to give you a name at last.*

"So you're sure it's Sunil?" I asked. I felt as if a weight had been lifted. No more tangled mysteries.

No more MRI or PET scans, Dad.

No more mention of AI.

It's all true.

As I dreamed it.

Wait till I tell the Bruhs of the Hexagonal Table about this! I thought. *Coming from Uncle Lennard I know they'll believe me. We'll have an example of a kid three hundred years ago learning to become a man, just as we are. I have to find out what his life was like. What he had to face. What lessons we can learn from him,*

"What about the shark attack?" I asked.

"Yes, that too. It happened. Skipper Jan Akkerman recorded it on one line in his log. That's why he offered Sunil the job on board as an ordinary seaman. His record says he was a Tamil pearl diver working in the Mannar Straits in the North during the season, even at his age, and delivering water to the ships in Galle during the off-season. That explains why he was such a good swimmer when he was diving for coins. With lungs like a blue whale."

"And the snake pit?"

"That one I can't be too sure about. My research confirms there was a hospital and a snake pit on São Tomé Island off

West Africa, but there's no record of Sunil visiting it when the *Zuytdorp* anchored there in 1711."

"Was the island *French*?" I interrupted him, sharply alert.

"At the time, yes, for a while. Most of the time it was run by the Portuguese."

I was right! My dreaming eyes were not deceiving me!

"So, what happened there? Why was the surgeon looking for extra medicines?"

"Many of the crew became ill there and died. Close to all of them according to the records in Cape Town. 112 of them by one report, passengers and crew, if I remember rightly. They caught malaria and had no defence against it."

"Yes, they did!" I burst out. "In my dream the surgeon was given some sort of tree bark to grind up and make a drink."

I picked up the first exercise book and flicked through it.

"Here it is. "Cinchona" bark. I wrote it down. I've never heard of it."

Uncle Lennard smiled. "That's slack of you, Suma. If you'd looked it up you'd know you can extract quinine from it and that's a cure."

I made a mental note to google everything I wasn't sure about in future.

"They had to recruit many men in Cape Town to make up the numbers. Many of them from the local prisons, apparently," Uncle Lennard said.

"What about the young bloke? The senior carpenter?" I asked.

He threw me a wide grin, leaned forward and with one elbow on the table, pointed his forefinger emphatically at his blue eye and shut the brown. "See this?" he said. "I reckon your young bloke was a shipwright called Gerrit de Waal. *My* ancestor this time."

"Your ancestor? How do you know?"

"Of course I don't know for certain, but I met him

everywhere in my research. As a young kid, related to his great-grandfather who captured the Portuguese ship the *Santiago* on St Helena Island in 1602, but that's another story. As an apprentice in the Middelburg shipyard in 1701, when he was fourteen, like you, where he worked on the *Zuytdorp* for six months. And as the senior carpenter aboard when she went down. I know that because we have a list of the people who signed on in Middelburg before she left in 1711 and he's on it. We don't have the list of the crew that left Cape Town on board later, because everything after that went down the gurgler with the ship."

"That doesn't make him your ancestor, does it?"

"No, but I've adopted him. I'm a glass sculptor. He's the same in wood. So why not?"

He had me there, and I nodded. "Makes sense to me, Uncle."

So, I thought, *Sunil Dewaraja and Gerrit de Waal. Now I know, and knowledge is power! Wait till I tell the bruhs about this.*

Uncle Lennard leaned forward and tapped the coin and the abalone pendant with his right forefinger. "My Mum Mary found these in a rusty tobacco tin at the back of a cave on the cliffs at Wanamalu Station," he said. "One of her Dachshunds had gone in there chasing a possum. You'd know the place, overlooking the Hutt Lagoon. Gerrit must have sheltered there. There are freshwater springs by the lagoon and it's a great spot to look out for passing ships. The tin was full of coins and some other relics. A pair of dividers. Silver buttons from an officer's coat. You name it. She took it to the Shipwrecks' Museum in Fremantle, but kept these and a couple of other coins. She gave them to me when I started researching the ship."

He picked up the coin, spun it in the air with a flick of his thumb, called heads as it landed on his palm and then showed me tails. "You win," he said. "They're yours for the time being, but they come back to me when you've finished with them."

"What do I do with them?"

"You're the psychic—or the would-be psychic—work it out. Experiment. Develop your psychic abilities. Maybe you wear the shell, hold the coin and use your skills to read the vibes they give you. What does that American kid on Netflix do? Tyler Henry. His cue to communicating with the dead is to scribble on a pad, if I remember rightly. These should serve the same purpose once you learn how to use them."

"What if they don't?"

"That's your problem, Suma. Then you find out what does work. It's not that your dreams aren't enough. It's one more string to your bow if it works, one more way of contacting them. And with our past. If it's Sunil trying to break through, which to me seems most likely, then we need to open the door for him. Like Rover Thomas did. We know the ancestors are all around us. We need to find out how best to listen to them."

I reached for the coin and wasn't surprised to discover it was Dutch.

It was a Zeeland *schelling*, minted in 1711, slightly bent and burred at the edges.

On one face, heads, I saw a crouching lion holding what looked like a hat balanced on the point of a sword. On the other, another lion, emerging on its back legs from the wavy sea embossed in a shield.

I handed it back to Uncle Lennard. "Can you explain what's these images mean?"

He pointed at heads. "The lion here was the symbol of the United Provinces, the Netherlands," he said, "and that's the hat of liberty on the end of the sword. Same as the hat Sunil was wearing—and you'll be wearing once you understand what it is you're discovering through your dreams."

He turned the coin over, "And this is the Zeeland coat of arms."

He handed it back to me, and for a moment I felt the weirdest tingling as I closed it in my fist, as if it was carrying the residue of everyone who had ever handled it in a faint charge of static electricity.

Even Gerrit de Waal, I thought. *He had touched it. Even him! And perhaps Sunil. You never know. And now me! Maybe I get the bruhs involved, get them to touch the coin as well and see if I'm imagining the static electricity. I can see Bones being sceptical. He always is. We'll see."*

The tingling alarmed me so much I dropped it quickly back on the table as if I'd been scorched, hoping Uncle Lennard hadn't noticed. I've never forgotten that first time I felt it. To this day, to be honest, even though I'm used to it now.

The slight lift of Uncle's left eyebrow and the hint of a brief smile told me he had, as he picked up his coffee, drained it to the dregs, wiped off the brown moustache it left on his upper lip and placed it deliberately back in the saucer. Then he leaned back, put his hands behind his head, stretched out and crossed his legs. For the first time I noticed his developing pot, but knew better than to comment.

"Now then," he said. "We've got the rest of the afternoon. Check out the menu for the best fish they've got here. Reorder the coffee and another milkshake. Then give me a blow-by-blow account of what you Bruhs of the Hexagonal Table, or whatever it is you call yourselves, got up to at the wreck site." He grinned. "In that order."

"That is what we call ourselves," I said, "and we're fulfilling our quest. Nothing's more certain."

We spent the rest of the afternoon enjoying fish and chips, washing it down with coffee and milkshake and talking about our quest to the cliffs, right down to the no longer extinct Greater Stick Rats' nests and Mozzie facing up to his phobias.

You know how all that went down over those three memorable days, so there's no point in reminding you. I don't need reminding either. It's tattooed into my memory, like the hexagon on my hip.

Before we parted, I had one question for Uncle Lenard that had been nagging at me ever since he mentioned Tyler Henry.

I turned to him as we stood to leave.

"You mentioned Tyler Henry, Uncle," I said. "He meets with many people he doesn't know and seems to get messages for them from dead relatives—and even living ones they've forgotten who are trying to contact them. If it works, should I try to do the same?"

"That's up to you, Suma, but my strong advice is no. Not at this stage. Don't get too ambitious. If you do, you may tap into things you don't want to see and that might shut down your gift altogether. You might see something you don't want to report. What do you do then? So take baby steps, by crikey. You can give me a call whenever you like, as you have been. I'm always available and happy to listen."

I walked with him to his beaten-up 2009 BMW in the car park, my mind buzzing and my body so light-footed I felt I was walking on air.

Chapter 11

IT TOOK ME A full week to discover how to get what I called my talismans, the coin and the pendant, to work for me.

When it happened it shook me.

I thought I might not come out of the trance—that's the best way to describe it—the same person I went in. Or come out of it at all.

It happened on the seventh day of my experimenting.

On Sunday, 27 April, 2024, at 8.15pm to be clear and precise.

In my room at the GG Boarding House College. Seated at my desk, with the curtains open and a view over the swimming pool, with its glimmering underwater lights turning the water into a three-dimensional block of aquamarine and silver.

I tried every combination for hours each night when I was alone, and nothing worked. Both talismans in my closed fists. On my open palms. With the pendant round my neck. The coin in my pocket. A candle lt. Unlit.

Facing all the cardinal points of the compass.

Eyes closed. Open.

You name it.

I began to wonder. *Is it because I'm unsure what I'll experience when it does work and won't recognise it? Have I given each combination enough time? Am I a dreamer who gets my visions when I'm asleep and out to it? Am I not a psychic of a different kind, like Rover Thomas, after all? I can already hear Bones taking the piss and Willie Mack having my back.*

I was beginning to wonder if I had the gift at all and was on the verge of giving up, when by sheer coincidence on the seventh evening I was putting the talismans away. I had the pendant hanging from my desk lamp. Its light was shining on the sea eagle gliding cross the swirl of blues and greens.

My top drawer was open, and I had the tingling coin in my right fist. I was about to drop it back in there.

When I looked at the sea eagle—my personal totem as you know—in the flash of an instant the shell expanded and took me with it.

I fought to control my shock, to observe what was happening as my consciousness seemed eerily to open up. I was on the surface of an infinitely growing sphere of glass, peering into a limitless space of which I was now a part.

How else can I explain it?

I looked down and saw myself hunched forward at my desk with my chin on my chest, and my eyes closed.

Other images then obscured my room and I faded from view. They were vague at first, like coloured smoke, as they swirled into view. And then, as if I was exerting my will over them in some way unfamiliar to me, they materialised into images of a raging sea and visions of a broken ship.

They were in the weirdest way a part of me, and I of them.

It was both terrifying and calming, both dizzying and clear as crystal.

All at the same time.

I saw Sunil Dewaraja wrenched across his upper bunk by the lurching ship.

I tensed and wondered what I was about to witness.

What lessons will I learn, to take back to the bruhs? The thought ran through my mind at once. *How will I describe Sunil's reaction to his predicament to them? Will his actions prove to us that he's one of our pathfinders? Which I'm already certain he is, in spite of Bones's dissing. If he doubts me one more time it really will be face off time, gloves or no gloves. Remember Johnny Elliott at your peril, Bones!*

Sunil was clinging to a bulkhead beam against which he had been flung as the ship screeched and tilted around him.

Tools hurtled from the storeroom shelves and barrels of bolts and nails flew sideways, scattering across the decking.

His red squeezebox was ripped apart beneath them.

He watched horrified, as I did, somehow reading his mind, as his cabin mate in the bunk below him ducked into a swinging masonry jack that bore down like a sledgehammer and crushed his skull.

Sunil gripped the beam above him as the violence of the ship's movements settled and she lay broached on her port side, the seas lifting and pounding her across the rocks.

From the deck below he heard the screams of crewmen trapped behind the battened hatches.

Somehow I was aware that the rows of cannons, shifted by the slewing of the ship, had wrenched from their ties and torn into her sides, and the sea was drowning all except the few who made it up the water-filled companionway ladders and through the narrow exits.

Sunil slid from his bunk and clambered to the sloping floor.

Once over his shock when the ship struck, he felt a growing calm, as if what was happening was in some way not unexpected. Was in the normal course of events for him, as if willed by the Hindu Lord Shiva in whom I realised he believed.

"*Om namah shivayah!*" I overheard him chanting over and over in a whisper. "*Om namah shivayah!*"

I could see he was prepared for what he had to do next.

He climbed against the steep angle of the deck, opened a wall locker and retrieved his ebony goggles. He slung them round his neck then reached deeper, for his hat.

His hat of liberty, Uncle Lennard had mentioned.

Liberty? How ironic, I remember thinking. *Another concept Twiga Gammie has drilled into us. Thank you Twiga!*

He bent to lift the cast iron jack from his cabin mate spread-eagled beneath it, but he was beyond help. He stepped sideways into the corridor and manoeuvred his way along the slant of the deck towards Gerrit's cabin.

The door swung inwards when he pushed it.

There was no sign of Gerrit at first. Then the ship shuddered once more, ground across the rocks, canted violently sideways and Gerrit's body slid from beneath his bunk. His arms were outstretched above his head, his seemingly lifeless face like wax beneath the foam.

Sunil caught him by the shoulders and pulled him into the passage, his body jerking wildly as he gasped and coughed, eyes closed, spouts of brown and bloody seawater spewing from his mouth.

Has he broken a rib and it's pierced his lung? I wondered. *No. He's bitten his tongue. At least he's breathing and he's conscious.*

The effort took agonising moments as Sunil's feet lost their grip and he slid across the deck, searching for a precarious hand or foothold as Gerrit's dead weight dragged him backwards into the cabin.

Gerrit lost consciousness before they reached the passageway. His breath was now a rasping moan. Then Sunil saw Gerrit's dangling and distorted right foot, the broken bone bulging beneath the torn skin pulsing blood. He reached out and felt the sickening shift of bone beneath his fingers.

He wedged Gerrit against the wall and crawled onto the midship deck where he clung to a dislodged rail, seeking an escape route for them both.

There he saw the extent of the disaster.

Waves smashed over the hull above him and swept deep across the deck, carrying wreckage in a swirl of foam. Between each thundering wave, he saw that the *Zuytdorp's* back was broken and the forepeak decking split.

Beneath him, the second deck was a surging flood. The masts were a mass of smashed and tangled rigging angled above the water boiling furiously round the hull. He saw shadows clinging to the spars. High on the rear deck a group of crewmen were struggling to release one of the ship's boats from its lashings.

He saw the rising shadows of cliffs through blinding rain.

He knew at once what he had to do.

He turned back down the passage, pausing to check on Gerrit, now dazed but conscious.

"I'll back in a moment, Gerrit," he shouted. "I'll help you. I'll check the forepeak to see if we can escape that way."

He worked his way towards the bows.

He climbed the short companionway to the heads, where he fought to open the door jammed shut by the wind. Then it swung open, and he saw that the platform at the bow beneath his feet was submerged, the sea surging through the gratings

Beyond it, the splintered bowsprit pole hung at right angles. It was smashed part-way along its length. The farther end was still attached to the ropes, and the small waterlogged staysail was entangled along its length.

As he watched, the bowsprit pole parted and the broken end swung wildly away across the face of a wave. It swept out the length of the rope that held it and then slid back on the inrush of the next wave and rammed the bow, just missing his legs.

He saw the dark shadows of broken wreckage swirling past and, much closer now, the looming cliffs.

He clambered back to the store to retrieve a knife sheathed to one of the canvas carpenter's belts and strapped it on.

Then he reached into the bamboo cage to grip his shrieking parakeet, before crawling along the passage to the bows. There he released it into the howling wind. It disappeared with a frantic whirr of wings into the darkness.

Then he squatted beside Gerrit in the shelter of the forepeak as the sea raged about them. Gerrit's dreadful injury he could do nothing about. There was no time to apply bandages or a splint. The ship was breaking up. He knew that the forepeak would separate and become engulfed. They'd collide with the cliffs within the hour, and with the storm directing its fury at the base of the cliffs they would stand no chance in the power of its surge. He knew the wild nature of the sea during monsoonal storms along the cliffs of Galle Fort Island, and they were tame compared to this.

"Our only option," he screamed at Gerrit, leaning in beside his ear, "is to risk jumping into the sea and trusting my instincts and swimming skills to find us a landing somewhere. If there is one. If not, we'll have to make it up the cliff-face."

Gerrit, fully conscious now, saw Sunil's determination and the ebony goggles at his throat. "You have to go without me, Sunil," he croaked. "That way you have a chance of surviving. Take me and we'll both drown. I'm done for anyway."

"If I survive without you that will be no survival." Sunil said.

He didn't wait for a reply.

He crawled rapidly out to the midship deck, where broken timbers screeched in the wind's relentless roar. There was no escape route that way now for certain. Across the gulf of surging water, he saw the ship was parting. The gunwales, high to his left, were split through as though cut with the swing of a gigantic axe.

"This is no time to argue," he shouted when he crawled back. "We go together, or we don't go at all. Neither of us."

"We'll both die, either way."

"So be it. We go together." He looked down at Gerrit. "The three of us."

He dragged Gerrit backwards by the armpits to the forward companionway and the door to the heads.

"You, me and my brother Vesak," he shouted.

Sunil leaned into the door and it swung open, a surge of water slamming it wide against the outer bulkhead. The platform was deeper now, water foaming through the railings.

The stump of the bowsprit pole reared into the driving rain.

He knelt beside Gerrit sprawled in the doorway, locked his arms around his chest and dragged him across the grating.

"You'll have to trust me, Gerrit," he screamed. "Don't fight me now, whatever happens."

He took out his knife and hacked apart the rope that was restraining the bowsprit pole.

He stood for one last deliberate moment, shouting a personal prayer into the wind: "*Om shrim hrim shrim Sarva mangalaya pingalaya om namah!*"

Then he launched himself across the railing and into the shock of the cold sea, hauling Gerrit with him into a thrashing wave that thrust them high and away from the forepeak.

They slid down the hollow of its backwash as the next wave roared in.

Sunil felt the current swirl around them, pulling them clear of the wreck.

He heard Gerrit's inhuman scream of pain and for a moment it was the remembered weight of Vesak he was fighting to keep above the raging water.

Above them, on the next surge, he saw the smashed bowsprit pole rolling in the wash and swinging towards them, the pale shadow of the torn staysail spread beneath it like a broken wing.

He struggled towards it and wrapped his free arm round a frayed rope.

They floated in the raging water for an hour, drifting slowly southwards on the current, with Gerrit slung across the smashed bowsprit pole. Sunil fought to keep him above the surface, wrestling with his dead weight as he slid away from the rotating timber when he lapsed into unconsciousness.

Unaware of the passing time, Sunil harboured his strength, his will concentrated on the effort to save his friend.

The broken ship had disappeared in the pelting rain behind them.

Alongside them, the cliffs towered into the storm-dark sky, lit eerily now and then by sheet lightning. The surf thundered and growled at their base, a sweep of white water foaming across the rock platforms as the waves burst across them.

Then Sunil saw a break in the cliffs.

The rock-face angled down towards a streak of sand, hidden as the waves crashed across it, pale as they swirled away. It was a momentary vision, a flash of white in the lightning. At its closest edge a shelf of rock stretched towards them in the roaring turbulence. Beyond it, the cliffs reared towards the skyline.

Unable to judge the distance and unsure of the strength of the current sweeping them down the coast and swirling across the wind, he knew that this was their last chance.

He grasped Gerrit across the chest, turned him over to face the sky, the foam breaking over the two of them, and then struggled away from the bowsprit pole, striking out for the spit of sand across the current.

He was dragged beneath Gerrit's inert form in his effort to keep him afloat, gulping air each time he surfaced.

He was no longer aware of the cliffs as he fought to reach them, conscious only of the wall of green water that washed around him as he sank, his lungs bursting, till he emerged choking in the rain and foam, to descend again into the wild green, his body straining towards the distant sand and safety, holding Gerrit's inert body up.

His struggle seemed to last forever.

The alternating wash of the sea and the roar of the wind.

The blinding wall of green.

His desperate gasp for air and his fight against drowning.

He was driven. He felt himself fainting, but forced himself to reach for the surface again. He sank into darkness but refused to abandon Gerrit. As he weakened, he retreated into a dazed red world in which his heartbeat roared, and his arms seemed torn away.

At last he felt the pull of the inshore undertow as it caught them, sucking them violently towards the rock platform and threatening to drag them into caverns beneath it.

In his agony he felt that this was one last danger they would not survive.

He had no answer to the sea's destructive force, and he clung to Gerrit as the waves hurled them towards the shelf.

He saw the shadow of the cliffs loom directly overhead. He saw the surf burst high around them. He heard the incoherent scream of the wind as they were thrown across the ledge, lacerated by its razored surface, the water surging over them.

He clung to the rock as the wave receded.

The next wave picked them up and tore Gerrit from his grasp as it drove them beyond the rock-shelf to hurl them across the sand. They rolled in the wash as another wave crashed about them, driving them further up the spit.

Gathering the last of his will, he crawled to Gerrit and dragged him beyond the breakers and past the debris and traces of seaweed at the tide line.

He stretched him out on the sand in the shelter of an overhang at the cliff face.

He listened for Gerrit's faint breathing, saw the bleeding lacerations and grimaced at the distorted angle of the broken bones beneath the skin above his ankle.

Gerrit was stirring.

Sunil forced himself to his feet to search at the cliff edge, where he found a length of grey driftwood. He snapped it in two and knelt to bind Gerrit's leg, using strips of his shirt and trouser leg. The bones ground beneath his fingers as he realigned them; and he bound the splints in place as Gerrit groaned before slumping into unconsciousness again.

With his back to the rock wall and exhaustion washing over him, Sunil felt a surge of triumph and relief. He looked towards the summit of the cliffs and at the dark sky beyond it. The stinging rain was easing. He felt a rush of gratitude to find himself alive as he gave himself over to fatigue, conscious that during his ordeal he had experienced an extraordinary state of mind in which his spirit, energised by his desperation, had extended the limits of his ability to endure.

He and Gerrit were alive.

His strength of will had carried them through.

He scraped two shallow pits in the sand, stretched Gerrit out in one and covered him in sand against the biting wind.

He lay shivering in the other. Still he could not sleep. He kept vigil as the storm raged on.

Towards morning the rain eased and the rim of the cliff behind him was gradually lit by the pale predawn, though the bitter wind still gusted over the sea from the south-west where further storm clouds were gathering.

When he looked at Gerrit, he saw him conscious and staring at the surging ocean.

"We've arrived," he said emerging from his pit and laying a hand on Gerrit's shoulder. "Now let me go and find out where."

He scrambled across the sand and then up the rock-slip where the cliff had fallen away.

Gerrit watched his shadow disappear across the summit.

For long, dazed moments he fought to bear the waves of pain each time he made the slightest movement. Lying still, cocooned in the blanket of sand, he watched the red rock-face behind him glimmer into life.

"I can tell you where, Sunil," he murmured. "Edel Land!"

As a boy he'd been fascinated by the discoveries others in the Dutch East India Company, the VOC, had made. He loved studying the charts and knew this coastline of cliffs in the continent of Nieuw Holland.

The rain drifted momentarily into a fine mist over him as the sun broke through the cloud and lifted over the summit. Far to seaward he saw black sheets of rain in storm fronts moving towards the shoreline; and one, struck by a shaft of sunlight, bore on its edge a rainbow briefly lit, its bands of colour wavering ghostlike and then snuffed out.

Was that a warning? Was it a hallucination?

He closed his eyes, stretched out his arms and opened his hands to the sun's welcome warmth.

And for me?

Emerging from the trance proved easier than I expected.

I simply willed it and jerked awake in my chair at the desk.

It was like waking from a dream, but more intense. Like dying in one place, and finding yourself alive a moment later in another, more familiar place. The curtains still open, the swimming pool lights now off. The abalone shell necklace still dangling innocuously—thank you, Twiga Gammie!—from the lamp.

I was still clutching the coin in my right fist. It left an indent in my palm.

And the clock? Showing 8.23pm. All that in eight long minutes.

Insane!

I couldn't wait to try again.

Tomorrow!

But most of all I was eager to tell the story to the bruhs, to let them know Sunil was truly one of us. *He has risked his life to save a friend,* I thought. *He was willing to die rather than abandon him. He has to be the seventh Bruh of the Septagonal*

Table now, just without the hexagon tattoo.
    And they all agreed.
    It was unanimous.

Chapter 12

ON THE LONG DRIVE back to Geraldton from the wreck site, Mozzie was unusually quiet. He looked as if he was brooding over what he'd achieved, the giant step he'd taken with that second confident leap into the pool. There was a subtle change in him, as if he was getting to know who he really was at long last.

"You okay back there, Mozzie?" Willie Mack asked, leaning forward in the front passenger seat to look at Mozzie in the rear-view mirror. "You did really, really well today, bruh. You didn't think, you thwam."

He was the fifth of eight brothers and an older sister, Ruthie. They lived in Kalbarri and Ruthie had looked after them all since their Italian mother died a year ago. He disappeared into the crowd because he was so quiet. I know, because I've been to his place and witnessed it. He was camouflaged by shyness. "He's so shy he doesn't know what to say when he's talking to himself," Willie Mack used to insist—far different from when he was with us, learning to speak his mind and use his fists.

His Wajarri Yamaji dad, Martin Buzzacott, operated a crayboat out of Kalbarri—the *Buzz Off*, a twenty-eight-foot Shark Cat. He ran his pots on his acreage along the cliffs from Red Bluff to Gregory, and on the reefs further out when the whites were on the summer run north towards deeper water.

With the earlier Covid lockdown and the Chinese crayfish export ban, though, the family had been suffering.

Badly.

His dad used to choose from among the older sons to work as his crew when he could afford the diesel and did go out, ignoring Mozzie, leaving him to blend with the wallpaper of their three-bedroomed house, except it was peeling green Dulux from a hundred years ago.

He had never been out on the boat.

How his dad afforded the fees for Mozzie to attend George Grey College I have no idea. Maybe someone in Primary School had recognised how goated Mozzie was in Maths and Science and he'd earned himself a scholarship. That was none of our business and we weren't about to ask. He was there with us and that was all that counted.

We didn't realise then how much publicity the film in Spanner's Mum's camera that day was about to score, let alone earn Mozzie the fees for the academic papers and newspaper articles that resulted.

Step aside the Tasmanian tiger!

Make way for Mozzie's Greater Stick Rat!

It was enough to put food and a change of menu on the Buzzacott table for at least the next six months.

But that's another episode altogether, so never mind Mozzie for now.

We had some fun and a few laughs at each other's expense on the long drive home that day. We took the piss and made up jokes about each other when we weren't singing.

This time Tiny had South Summit's *Tales of the Yeti* songs on the Bluetooth stereo Spanner had installed. We had it blaring at first, our discordant voices echoing, before we turned it off. We'd selected South Summit for the trip, because their songs slap and Mozzie was their first enthusiastic fan among us. Besides, we had a connection with them when we were aboard *Quixote II* and heard them at the Spring by the Sea Festival in 2022, when the Alpha Bruhs were born.

It was Willie Mack's idea to crack some jokes, after several minutes' silence in a particularly rocky stretch of road. We had to slow down, and I was absorbed in admiring the glowing Banksias from my left-hand seat in the back. Tiny was taking it easy to avoid the tyres getting staked, but we were still lurching from side to side, packed into the Wrangler like a gazillion refugees caught in a cyclone in a rubber ducky.

"Enough of this silence, bruhs," Willie said, his voice going up and down with the movement of the Wrangler. "Time for a laugh. Here's one for starters. It's about you, Mozzie." He was clearly trying to lighten Mozzie's mood and draw him into the conversation. "Why doesn't Mozzie want to become an accountant when he grows up?"

"I don't know. Why?" Bones said.

"Because he doesn't want to spend the rest of his life counting the cost."

That scored two blue beans when the groans and laughter died down.

Willie Mack kept the blue bean score in the little note book he was always scribbling in, to be delivered on our right shoulders when we reached Murchison House Station. We ended up with so many our arms were paralysed when we got home.

I remember a few of the jokes. Most were corny, some hit the spot and others I wouldn't repeat to my Mum.

Or to you.

Let me tell you a few.

Willie then said, "Your turn, Bones."

But Spanner broke in instead.

"Why is Willie Mack, the Pom, like a haemorrhoid?"

Silence.

"Because he's a pain in the arse, sticks out like a dog's and won't go back where he came from."

"Hey, Racism! At last!" Bones said. "There should be more of it!"

"A *Pom?*" Willie Mack said with a laugh. "I'll have you know I'm a purebred Australian Scot of the clan Maclean from the land of milk and honey and you salute when you're in my presence."

"Yeah, one finger," Spanner said.

Two blue beans.

"If Summer's got second sight," Tiny broke in for the first time in a while and silenced us, shock like a block of ice suddenly melting in my gut, "why did he give up astrology?"

"Because he discovered there's no future in it," Willie Mack said. He'd heard it before. "That's an oldie but a goldie, Tiny. Nice try."

No blue beans. Not for Tiny.

"What did Spanner say to the old woman whose car broke down on Anzac Terrace and he walked over to help her?" Bones said. "True story. I was with him."

That one we all knew.

""Are you telling me your engine's missing, Aunty?" he asked her, head down and bum up under the bonnet. "Then how did you get here?"" Bones said.

"Hey, Mozzie," Willie Mack said a little later, "Think of a word and we'll make up jokes about it."

Mozzie did not respond at once, and then, "Music. How's that?"

"Music. That'll do," Willie Mack said.

"It's a roughie and a toughie," Bones said, after several minutes' puzzled silence, before his face lit up. "I've got one! What do old musicians do when they die?"

"I have no idea," Willie Mack said, his ginger eyebrows raised as he peered back at us over the front seat.

"They decompose!" Bones yelled. He was so excited I was worried he'd let one go and suffocate us all with his variation on poison gas, even though we had the roof off.

Willie Mack came back with, "Why did Beethoven go deaf playing his piano?"

"Why?" Bones obliged.

"Because his mind wasn't sound and he played it by ear."

The first three blue bean joke.

"Why do we hate listening to Bones singing?" I asked.

It was true. We couldn't stand it. He couldn't hold a tune and was always flat as a four-day roadkill fox. You didn't want to be beside him when we were going for it with the Bluetooth blaring.

I didn't wait.

"Because he's tone deaf and we wish we were stone deaf."

One blue bean, but Willie Mack liked it.

"Good one, Summer," he said. "Old Twiga's rubbing off! As for Bones's singing, he thinks it's as easy as shelling peas but finds it as difficult as peeing shells—and sounds like it."

"Yeeeeouch!" Bones yelled. "Let's think of another word. Sex! How's about that?"

Here we go, I thought. *Bones and Spanner, in their element.*

All the dick jokes that followed are off the table, even though we pissed ourselves laughing at them as the air turned blue, and not from one of Bones's farts.

Sorry about that, if you're disappointed.

It's not that I'm salty about it, but I don't want you to think a dick joke is the highlight of my story and remember nothing else, to be honest.

When Spanner'd got the last one out and things went quiet, Mozzie suddenly piped up, "What makes Bones tick?"

"*What?*" Bones asked. "What makes me tick?"

"No brains," Mozzie giggled. "You're tick as a brick."

At last the youngest of us all had rejoined us, and for that, no blue beans.

"Right on, Moz!" Tiny said. "That's why his parents need to send him in for a CT scan."

"Hey, bruhs. I seem to be the one copping shit today. Pick on someone else, why don't you!"

"It's because your mouth's always arriving while whatever brains you *do* have are still getting in the taxi," Willie Mack said. "You admitted that when Summer took you outside that time."

"Water off a duck's back, *smartarse!*" Bones said.

"Why did Spanner's folks build their house with mud bricks?" I asked, to ease the rising tension.

"And why is *that?*" Spanner asked abruptly. I sensed his alertness. Fight or flight, he always stiffened protectively whenever anyone mentioned his folks.

"Because they're dirt cheap," I said.

"Three blue beans," Tiny said, turning round to look at me with a smile. He turned back to his steering. "What happened to Summer when he met Charlie Marks at a séance?" he asked.

I felt my heart give a sudden lurch and my face flushed. I was glad I had brown skin, but knew my eyes would give me away, so I stared out at the passing Banksias.

I've never mentioned Charlie to anyone. I thought. *What does Tiny know that I don't? Why did he pick Charlie of all the girls in Edith Cowan House?*

"What happened?" I managed to ask, trying to keep my voice level and unconcerned, but hearing it come out a little hoarse.

"It was love at second sight, of course." He chuckled. "I reckon that's right on the money."

"It most certainly is," Willie Mack said. "And it's an interesting observation. Here's another. Why does Summer think Charlie Marks is like a stick of dynamite?"

No one answered.

I gazed at the passing trees, barely noticing them.

"Because she wears her hair in a *BANG!*"

"What's a bang?" Bones asked.

"A fringe, like Charlie's."

Traitors!

That had everyone laughing at my expense. I had no option but to join in, but felt myself cringe inside, too charged up to think of a reply and unwilling to give the game away.

I was relieved when we rattled over the bridge across the river at last and I saw the shadow of Murchison House Station looming to our right, the setting sun lighting up the western sky in a blazing orange and scarlet wash.

We parked up the Wrangler and with the engine still running we divvied up the blue beans.

It was a free-for-all.

"Hey, Mozzie," Willie Mack said, as Tiny hit the road again in the fading light. "What are we humans made up of?"

"The particles of exploded supernovas," Mozzie said. "Maybe more than one."

"I thought so. If I'm the ashes of a dead star, I hope I'm Elvis." He leaned across and looked back at us. "How's about some karaoke?"

The next moment we were singing "Hound Dog" at the top of our voices as Tiny dropped three of us off at the places we were staying that night, and it was "Blue Suede Shoes" when Tiny, Mozzie and I arrived at the GG Boarders' College. We knew them because we'd sung Presley songs that Friday evening at the karaoke session in the common room with some girls from Edith Cowan House. I left early because Charlie Marks wasn't there.

"Meringue" Utting had allowed us a week's stay beyond the end of term.

Meringue Utting, you ask? Who the hell is he?

She, actually. She's the Matron of the Boarders' College, been here for years. She's German, at least sixty, has this cropped red hair with grey roots and is very old school, like Twiga. But she's fit and built, does weights and uses the rowing machine in the gym. She has these piercing blue eyes that never miss a trick. You don't mess with her, unless you want the short hairs on the back of your head pulled sharply upwards when she's disciplining you. Makes your eyes water, but you don't complain or it lasts longer.

And *Meringue?*

Easy. She's the opposite of sweet, for starters. She's definitely sour, and her Christian name is Merryn. So it's a slam dunk as the old saying goes.

But there's more.

Willie Mack, who's convinced she's Hitler's second cousin once removed and was a guard at Belsen or Buchenwald, preferred "Orang", as in Orangutan—considering her surname, her size and the colour of her hair.

When we put it to the vote, he lost.

Which is rare as Tasmanian tiger shit for him.

Meringue-utan sounded good to us and it stuck, though we dropped the –utan suffix because the full name was too much of a mouthful when we started using it.

Chapter 13

THE NEXT NIGHT, ON the Monday, I set up the talismans and my room exactly as they'd been the night before. Right down to the time, the open curtains, the swimming pool lights and the drawer. I went as far as eating the same meal in the dining room, in case that had some influence, and wearing the same clothes despite of the rank smell of armpit sweat.

I was aware that the experience happened last time without me doing anything consciously to start it.

This was different.

I was hyped.

Self-conscious and apprehensive.

Keen to succeed. Doubtful whether I would.

I was so wary my mind was filled with as many negative thoughts as positive. *Was last time a fluke? Am I really a psychic? Surely, I am. It was so vivid. Or had I somehow fallen into a catnap and dreamed up the whole of the rescue? I could already hear Bones's insulting jeers.*

Anyway.

This is what happened.

Things got off to a flying start without my say so.

The shell expanded like an infinite glass sphere as it had before, with me tapping into some sort of weird universal consciousness across its infinite space but keeping my sense of self at the same time.

I saw me at first, hunched over at the desk, and the same smoky swirl of blurred images that blotted out my room as I willed them to form.

But what appeared was very different.

The *Zuytdorp*? Yes. But this time on a flat, still sea so blue it mirrored the ship drifting on its own reflection.

Was she anchored?

No.

Slight ripples showed behind her as she barely moved, the lightest of now-and-then breezes nudging her, a green hula-skirt of weed at the waterline shifting and waving below the surface, emerging here and there to take the sun.

The image strengthened, like it was a colour photograph emerging in a bath of developing fluids, and I found myself participating in a ceremony on the mid-ship deck.

And then I saw Sunil.

I was immediately alert, on edge. *What am I gunna report to the bruhs this time?* I wondered. *I'll have to remember every detail.*

He was with two others; each lashed to a chair beside the rail. His parakeet was tied to a leg of the chair, the tether long enough for it to perch behind him on the chair back.

He was younger. He wasn't wearing a shirt. His scars were like a series of pink and red steps up his chest, raw beside his dark skin. The ship's barber had lathered his head and shaved it. A foaming mess of hair and white slops lay at his feet, the barber's bare footsteps slipping in it as he shoved it aside.

Three new grey felt hats hung on hooks at the rail.

Three hats of liberty, I realised.

Aha!

It was the crossing of the equator!

Bearded skipper Jan Akkerman was standing in for King Neptune, with his officers and the crew permitted this time to knock back tankards of beer and glasses of rum to celebrate rounding Cape Good Hope—and for reaching the equator off the Brazilian *Abrolhos Shoals* without a serious incident.

A sailor opened the gate in the rails and unrolled a rope ladder down the side, as another untied the three bald victims covered in lather. They had never crossed the equator before.

They were led in single file to the gate.

Then they were pushed over the side and into the sea without ceremony to clear the soap, prodded in the backside with a deck scrubbing broom. The crew raised a glass and cheered, some whooping drunkenly as each of them fell in, the giant Bo'sun fingering a whip at his belt eyeing the drunkards off.

Two of them reappeared, spluttering, thrashed their way to the wood-rung ladder and clambered back up to the deck.

The skipper congratulated them and handed each his hat.

But there was no sign of Sunil.

A minute passed.

Two.

Three.

Not four, surely?

Four!

The crew lined the rail and peered over it.

I sensed the growing panic among the officers and the concern of the sailors leaning over the rail peering at the sun-reflecting water blinding in the calm, with a hand shading their eyes.

A drowning? Another shark attack? Not *Sunil* this time, surely. Not after his brother.

One of the officers ordered two of the better swimmers to leap in and dive for him. As they did so, there he was, strolling unconcerned and silent from the other side of the ship, his wet footsteps leaving a trail across the deck.

He joined the others at the rail.

"You looking for me?" he asked.

They turned as a group and there was uproar and laughter. Four sailors grabbed him by his arms and legs, swung him three times with pig gibberish shouts of "Één," "*Twee*," "*Drie*" at the gate and hurled him as far as possible out into the sea.

He swivelled round in mid-air.

I saw him gulp in a great breath before he hit the surface,

dive and repeat the performance. He took his time and emerged on the other side, where he climbed the iron ladder rungs.

I saw the faint scratches on his back where he'd misjudged his depth and scraped the barnacles on the hull. They weren't bleeding and didn't seem to worry him.

When skipper Jan Akkerman presented him with the hat, I recalled the bumblebees that had struck its brim in my earlier dream, and as if that was a cue to waking up without me willing it, I was back in my room as if I'd stepped through a waterfall without getting wet.

I lurched upright.

It was 8.18pm.

A three-minute vision, this time.

Short and sweet.

I didn't have a say in the matter—but I did have a say with the bruhs at the next meeting.

They were all ears, and Tiny's "Good one Summer, that's right on the money!" when I'd finished meant the world to me.

Our seventh bruh, I thought, *has given us an example of how we should use whatever skills we have to our advantage, to make it count. To make sure we sharpen our gifts into a fine art and deliver the result to the world with a sense of humour and honour—and never, ever rawdog it. Tiny with his leadership skills. Spanner with his mechanical and engineering abilities. Bones with his running and athletic prowess. Willie Mack as a writer. Mozzie with his interest in the Sciences and his grasp of Maths. And me with my art.*

Me with my art?

That night I knew I had to take the next step. I had to graduate from pastels to acrylics and oils. I'd talk to Cormac about it. And as I realised that, I felt glow spread across my chest. I'll dedicate my first painting to Charlie Marks, no matter what the bruhs or anyone else says or thinks. That way I'll have an opportunity to talk to her.

Heart to heart.

Oh, *yes!*

I can still see the trail of Sunil's wet footprints across the deck. The sunlight of the passing years will never dry them in my memory.

I have to follow them, I realised.

Chapter 14

I WAS WOKEN BEFORE dawn the next morning by someone splashing in the swimming pool. My alarm clock read 4.31am.

What the hell is going on? I wondered, yawning. *Who's in there? Some sped? Not the school's swimming team. Their comps are over and they're on a break. A dog has fallen in, maybe? A roo? Don't be absurd! But hang on. We did have one wander into the grounds last year. One of Aunty Millie Sand's joeys from her roadkill rescue pound down the road. The truckies and tourists bring them in. She's usually got a dozen or more she's caring for. The girls in Cowan House went nuts for it before they took it back.*

I looked out into the shadows round the pool, dimly lit by the night lights.

Someone was doing doggie paddle down its length.

With difficulty.

All arms and legs.

So uncoordinated it would have been funny if it hadn't give the impression of someone drowning.

Drowning?

At *this* time of the morning, for god's sake?

Surely not.

I could see the foam and the shadow as the swimmer struggled to complete the length, he or she splashing so desperately I thought they'd never make it. At one point the shadow trod water, and even that was difficult, spinning slowly round on the spot before thrashing on. But the shadow reached the end and sat on the steps there, so obviously dead tired I could hear the coughing and the gasping intakes of breath from here, even with the window shut.

And then, I couldn't believe it, the shadow started out on a return leg, struggling to come up for air with each stroke.

Doggie paddle? No, that's someone trying to do overarm and hasn't got a clue, I realised. *The dickhead is definitely gunna drown.*

Pissed off but curious, I resigned myself, threw the sheet off and swung out of bed. I turned on my desk lamp, reached for the pendant and put the sea eagle to my lips for a moment, as I'd been doing each day first thing since I'd had it. No harm in starting off on the right foot with your totem.

Then I put my boardies on and went out to the pool.

To my surprise it was Mozzie.

He was out to it.

He was hanging off the side now, his lungs going like the clappers, so much like a panicking asthmatic I could hear the wheezing deep in his throat.

I sat down on the pool's edge beside him, my legs in the water. It was cold, but not cold enough to freeze your balls off.

"What the frick are you doing, Mozzie?" I asked him. "You should be asleep and so should I. You'll wake everyone in the house and they'll come out and drown you."

"What's it look like, Summer?" He could barely get the words out. "You guys can all swim. I'm the odd one out. It pisses me off."

"So, you've decided to learn freestyle at *this* time of day? What's wrong with you, bruh?" I said. I was so concerned for him I heard my voice crack, as if I was reprimanding him and didn't mean to. "You're one of us. You only have to ask. You should know that. Remember the code. We have each other's backs. We'll teach you. In the right place at the right time. You don't have to drown at 4.31am doing it on your own so we all end up wearing a black armband for you." I frowned down at him. "How long have you been out here?"

"Since three o'clock. I've been doing it for the past three days. You're the first one who's taken any notice."

"*Jeeeesus*, Mozzie! You deserve a medal, but I'm not going

to give you one. You woke me up, you little shithead." Then I relaxed and grinned. "Okay, just this once. I can't believe I'm saying this at this fricking hour, but since you're so keen I'll come in with you and give you your first lesson. But that will be it, bruh. From here on, we do it right. Out at Lucky Bay in the lagoon behind the reef. In the sun. With the tinny standing by and Bazza giving you some bloody encouragement."

I slipped into the pool, turned him round face down, hooked his feet in the drain at the edge and guided him through the stroke. The awkward position forced him into using it to keep his face out of the water, breathing on alternate sides without going anywhere. I took up the same position beside him and did the same. Clumsy and desperate at first, he soon got the hang of it and settled. Then we turned round, held the side and churned the water with our legs going full bore, like the propeller of the Johnson 25. We did that for half an hour, alternately, before I decided we'd had enough.

"Okay, Mozzie," I said. "Lesson one in Freestyle 101 is over. Time to clean our teeth and head for breakfast. No more of this travelling solo bullshit. We're six individuals forming a single unit and don't you forget it."

Within a month he could struggle through the full kilometre of the Lucky Bay Lagoon, like he was crossing the Tasman to New Zealand with the five of us swimming beside him, and within two he was night diving with us for crays outside the reef, even though it was against the rules—one of the rules we *could* break according to our code, by the way, if it helped us achieve our goals.

In this case the goal was Loyalty.

Bones surprised us all one afternoon, when Mozzie proved his swimming skills were not far off ours.

"Green's your colour, Mozzie, isn't it?" he asked "At least that's the colour of your tatt."

"Yep. Always has been. Why?"

"I'd like to present you with this."

He stepped forward and pulled from his pocket a green satin ribbon with a medal hanging from it. The medal was simply embossed, *Mozzie* and *Swimmer 2024*, with a swimming figure doing freestyle between the words. On the back was a hexagon.

Bones had gone out of his way to get Julie May, the jeweller at Marlon Craker's to cast it for him, using aluminium.

Mozzie thanked him and we all congratulated Bones for his thoughtful loyalty.

"Thank you, Bones."

"Good one."

"Well done, bruh."

"You deserve it, Mozzie! You've graduated from swimming 101."

"Right on the money, Bones."

Chapter 15

WITHIN A WEEK I was back beneath the cliffs on the spit of sand in my trance.

I was getting the hang of the starting technique—it needed only the two talismans after all, and it worked at any time of day, requiring a level of deep concentration I was learning to apply.

But only one in three sessions resulted in images, I discovered.

There were times when I found myself staring into empty space and tried again, several times. On the first occasion it was like I was trying to start a car that wouldn't crank up, and I was panicking because I didn't know if it was a dud starter motor or the battery was running low. *This is when I call on Spanner for his opinion and a fix, bruh!* I remember thinking as I tried again.

Anyway.

There I was, looking at Gerrit, who I knew was realising that this wild dawn was his first step on a journey into uncharted territory, calling for all his courage, resilience and will. I sensed his gut-wrenching rush of dread as he wondered what challenges and dangers lay ahead. Gritting his teeth against the pain, he dragged himself from the sand and shifted closer to the cliff face.

Leaning back against a rock part-sheltered beneath the canopy of an overhang, he saw his trouser leg was cut away and his throbbing lower right leg was crudely bound to driftwood splints. It was inflamed and the flesh was swollen, bulging red and blue between the ties. His left leg was also badly bruised and lacerated.

He glanced across the sand as stinging rain pelted down once more in driving wind.

Eyes tight shut, he tilted up his face with his mouth wide open to gather water funnelling from the lip of the overhang.

When he opened them, he found himself looking directly into the concerned, exhausted faces of Sunil and the officer I'd seen in the dream in Middelburg.

They were leaning over him.

"Good morning, Joost," he groaned, "and Sunil." He attempted a smile, but all it did was crack the film of salt caked on his cheeks. "Fancy meeting you here. What a coincidence."

"Morning, Gerrit," Joost replied. "It's good to see you among the living. It seems we miscalculated our position. Badly. Now we have a situation. We're going to need you."

"Ready and willing, but how useful I'll be with this leg is another matter. How many survivors are there?"

"Fifteen or so at my last count. There are bound to be more by the time we get back. Most were caught between decks and must have drowned."

"Any sign of skipper Marinus? And the other officers?"

"No. Neither him nor any of the others. Just you and I to deal with the situation, and you aren't in the best shape. Let's get you up to join us for a start.'

"Up *there?*" Gerrit pointed a thumb across his shoulder at the slope of rock. "I hope you're joking."

Grunting, they heaved his dead weight upright.

His pale, salt-and-sand encrusted face twisted, and he let out an unearthly groan as the pressure of the blood-flow rushed through the wound. It took several minutes to stabilise before he could move.

Then, supporting him on either side, he began the painful trek, struggling to hop on his bruised left leg and swing his right foot forward with each stride, the bones grinding agonisingly together as he took each step.

An hour later, after a climb up the slope and across the saltbush heath at the clifftop, with Gerrit swamped by waves of pain, dry-reaching and often on the verge of fainting, they joined the scattered group.

They supported Gerrit for a moment as he peered down at the broached wreck below them. It was broken into three. Its shattered main and mizzen masts hung over the rock-shelf across which successive breakers crashed and seethed, tossing the wreckage and corpses of sailors and sheep in the boiling cauldron between the smashed hull and the cliffs.

Then they led him hopping to the shelter of a cluster of Ti trees across which the survivors had earlier tied a square of salvaged sailcloth, another as a windbreak.

Three crewmen lay asleep beneath it.

Sunil cleared a patch of sand beside them for Gerrit to do the same.

As they carefully stretched him out, Gerrit grasped Sunil's hand.

"Thank you, Sunil. I will find a way to repay you… even if it's with the life I owe you," he said.

"There's no need for that, my friend" Sunil replied. "I did for you what I should have done for Vesak. You have repaid me already."

Joost's face turned grim as he gestured at Gerrit's wounds. "You may not thank Sunil for what we must do to you now, Gerrit. We need to reset your leg. It will not heal at that angle." He handed Gerrit a chunk of wood he'd selected. "You may want to bite on this."

Later that day, with Gerrit's leg straightened and tightly bound, Sunil squatted beside him and described what he'd discovered when he reached the wreck site.

He found a scene of devastation, he said. Much the same as it was now.

A dozen or so dazed and exhausted men had gathered at the lip of the boulder strewn cliff above the wreck. Some were standing, others in a state of collapse, staring down at the stricken wreck. Most were bleeding from lacerations they received when they scrambled barefoot over the rock platform beneath the summit.

Among them was a woman, a passenger Sunil recognised, hysterical, her three children he had often entertained, now gone.

He joined the traumatised group and looked down to see two men clinging to the stays, edging their way across the smashed mainmast towards the cliffs. The second man he recognised. It was Joost de Vlieger, still in his blue-coated uniform, his red hair plastered to his skull, a crammed black leather satchel strapped across his back.

Beyond them was another man teetering on the foremast, who overbalanced and mistimed his last-minute leap to safety. He fell screaming into a retreating wave that caught him up and thrust him backwards into foam boiling into caverns beneath the shelf. His torn body was unrecognisable when it was spat out minutes later to join others rolling in the raging surf.

When Joost leaped to the shelf and clambered up to them at last, he acknowledged each survivor in turn, though he wasn't familiar with them all, before he collapsed exhausted on the rocks and looked down at the chaotic scene below.

Then he turned and looking up at Sunil, gestured at the wreck. "Gerrit?" he asked.

"No, we're both ashore." Sunil pointed south. "He's on a beach a short walk down there. He has a badly injured leg. I'll need help to bring him up here."

"We'll need him. Give me time. We'll do it together."

"The rain won't last," Sunil said. "We're going to need water once it passes," He glanced northwards at the gulley two hundred metres beyond them running eastwards at right angles from the cliffs. "While you're resting, I'll take a look around."

He made his way across to the gulley and down its slope.

He followed the sand and limestone floor inland through windblown stands of trees he didn't recognise.

Then he splashed through rainwater leaching like sweat through the limestone slope, and half a kilometre inland he found what he what he was searching for—several seepages from a seam of denser rock at eye level below the gulley's rim.

As he and Vesak used to do on the Ulawatte hillside in Galle on their way to school after the monsoon rains, he cupped his hands and drank.

As if he's drinking from a soda fountain, I thought as I watched

And then, beyond the dribbling water, he tracked the seam as it ran wavelike through the rock-wall before curving downwards. At its end he discovered a naturally excavated hollow, a cylindrical pit part-filled with clear water, a metre across and elbow-deep.

Elated, he dragged a loose boulder across it, to conceal his find from animals and shelter it from the sun before he made his way back to Joost.

He hoped there'd be more seams and catchment pits further down the gulley, or in others further north.

Perhaps it was the discovery of the gnamma hole filled with water or the flowing seepage he drank from, but my vision was over, and I was out through the waterfall and back in my room.

So Sunil and Gerrit did survive.

They were on the clifftop and at least had a limited supply of water.

I was impatient for the next vision.

So were the bruhs after I described this instalment to them.

It was like waiting for the next episode or series 2 of a historical documentary on Netflix, Binge or Disney Plus that can't come fast enough for us.

Including Bones! Now there's a miracle! I thought. *He listened for once and didn't make a comment. What's turned the sceptic around? Is he getting soft in his old age? He'd better not. The state cross country finals are next week and the National Track events for Little Athletic runners is on in mid-October in Brisbane. If the 2032 Olympics with him in the green and gold are his goal, he doesn't need to soften up now.*

Chapter 16

IFIRED UP THE starting technique the next night and was immediately surprised to find myself back on the clifftops with Sunil, Gerrit, Joost and the other survivors—all 26 of them as it turned out.

Somehow I knew it was June 20, 1712, as I took in the scene—three weeks since the shipwreck.

It was late evening. The rising moon was full and bright, lighting up a cloudless blue-green sky. There'd been no rain since the storm, and none was threatening. The smoky signal fire was a roaring mass of flames three metres high, bedded on glowing embers at the cliff edge. Sparks were rushing skyward in the updraft like swarms of angry bees.

A large pile of thick green branches lay beside it.

I noticed as the image sharpened that the woman passenger was no longer among the survivors, and I saw her in sudden flashback hurl herself off the cliff at its highest point on the second night. She was clearly unable to bear the loss of her husband and her kids, let alone survive among starving sailors drunk on gin they'd salvaged from the wreck

There'd been no sign of any ships passing.

Joost was squatting beside Gerrit.

He gestured at the blazing fire and I overheard him say, "If any skipper saw our signal during the night or the smoke during the day, with these cliffs I'm certain there is nothing on this earth would convince him to come close enough inshore to check. If I was in his place, I'd do the same—sail on!"

"Where does that leave us, then?"

"We have no other option. We will move the campsite north beyond the cliffs, and the sooner the better. The beaches opposite Dirk Hartog Island provide far better access to the open sea."

Gerrit pointed at his healing leg. "Where does that leave me?"

"I won't abandon you here to take your chances, my friend. We will make a stretcher and carry you."

"And be a burden to you? Slow you down. No. I choose to stay here, and Sunil with me. We've discussed this possibility and he has agreed." He tapped his temple with a forefinger. "I've had an idea up here for some time. A signal so surprising any passing skipper will consider it a message sent to him directly from Paradise. They'll talk about it in Batavia and Middelburg for years to come. A gigantic kite! We send it aloft, and then we explode it."

Joost slowly nodded. "That's brilliant! A Chinese rocket. But how would you construct it? And launch it? And set the charges?"

Gerrit waved a hand around the campsite. "We have the sailcloth. We have the ropes. We have the linseed oil salvaged from the wreck. We have sufficient gunpowder left in the barrel that came ashore. And we have hands and time to spare."

Joost sat back and nodded. "Right, then we should get it done. You have three days, Gerrit. We will leave then, travelling at night to avoid the heat, while the moon is full."

Within a day, following Gerrit's instructions, Sunil and another two survivors prepared the necessary parts. Intact sailcloth cut to a diamond shape, three metres long and half as wide. A strong but slender green tree trunk heated in the fire and straightened for the spine, its branches trimmed and bowed for the spars and lower reinforcing ribs. A three-line sheet unravelled for the ties and the cord, and a long shank of flayed rope for the tail.

They took a further day and a half to assemble it, before successfully testing it in flight at the clifftop on the strong afternoon breeze. Then they applied linseed oil to the body and tail in preparation for impregnating it with gunpowder before launching.

"All you need now are passing ships," Joost said, when he was organising the departure. "Are you sure your ignition system is foolproof?"

"We can only use it once," Gerrit replied, "so it had better be. We'll know when we see any sails out there and launch it. We've bowed the spars, so the tail is not needed for its balance in flight. It will make a perfect fuse once we light it. The kite will fly until the flame reaches it and then, guess what?" he violently clapped his hands. "*Kaboom!*"

"You hope."

"I know."

"You've done this before?"

"No."

"I like your confidence."

"Trust me. You have so far. I am your senior carpenter, after all."

"All right then, we'll give it one more day. If the signal fails or we sight no ships we must move on."

"Without me."

"Without you, if that's your final word."

"It is."

"Food and water?"

"Water we have. Sunil knows where to find it. For food, we are well supplied. He's dived for those red lobsters here when it was calm for those two days, as you know. We have the fish he catches with the hooks he fashioned from nails when he dived into the wreck. We have oysters. And we have the rats here, when we can learn to catch them."

Joost nodded. "Gourmet meals, Gerrit. I will think of you when I have to make do and chew another strip of salted mutton. Before we leave, I'll make sure we remove one of the wooden statuettes of the Grecian sphinx from the rear transom and leave it within view, partway up the cliff. That will give you something to remember us by."

"And anyone who discovers this place in the future will know we've been here," Gerrit said.

"They will indeed."

Joost and his crew left that night.

Three days later, late in the afternoon when Gerrit was asleep, Sunil sighted a sail on the horizon.

"Gerrit!" he screamed, waking him. "There is a ship!"

Gerrit struggled to sit up and focus. The sail looked like an unearthly mirage, before another two followed closely, line abreast.

"Get the gunpowder!" he said. "Prime the kite. We don't have long."

Sunil splashed the remains of the linseed oil across the sailcloth and soaked the tail, then he poured gunpowder across both. He unwound the cord to its full length, running it in a series of loops across an open area of heath between the campsite and the cliffs, its end bound to a boulder at the cliff edge.

He lifted the kite, walked to the lip of the cliff beside the fire, and waited for Gerrit's signal.

That took twenty minutes, as the ships came straight on before the wind, then jibed away to port to begin their broad reach to the north-west.

Gerrit's shout was hoarse. "*Now*, Sunil. Now's the time. Fire away!"

"We need more wind."

"It's strong enough. There's no time to waste. Let it fly!"

Holding the kite head high, its ribs bending as the wind caught it, Sunil worked the thrashing tail across the fire. It crackled into flame and he released the kite, allowing the cord to unravel across both palms, applying pressure as the kite lifted and dipped and shook violently, struggling for height, before soaring across the campsite and powering upwards, gyrating to the left and then the right as he fought to manage it.

Dragged slowly across the heath as the cord ran out, Sunil released it as the last loop hissed across the sand.

It gave out a loud *thwack* as the tie at the boulder held.

For several minutes, the cord hummed like a piano wire before it snapped, sending the kite zigzagging wildly across the sky as though attempting to escape the flame ascending towards it.

Then the sailcloth exploded, spitting fire in orange and yellow flames before plunging towards the ground. A trail of thick black smoke marked its descent, as if someone had thrown a tin of paint across the sky's clear blue.

Arm-waving Sunil leapt and screamed along the lip of the cliff, but to his frustration, fury and despair, the ships sailed on.

Gerrit's kite signal had failed.

Will there ever be an end to their bad luck? I wondered as I watched. *It's easy to sense and share in their despair. What will they do now?*

The next afternoon, Sunil took the empty water canister and made his way to the second pool in the gully to the north.

As I observed, it hadn't rained for several days, and then only briefly.

It was clear the seepages were drying up, so for the past week, Sunil had been refilling the water canister more sparingly than usual.

At the pool, he half-filled the canister and then, on an impulse, he left it there and walked farther up the gulley in search of other pools. He found none, eventually reaching its end, its sides closing in and the floor sloping upwards.

He climbed to an exposed grassy clearing and stood among the green thickets at its edge, watching a mob of grey animals similar to those he'd sighted once or twice inland from the campsite. Alerted to his movement or his presence on the wind, they bounded away on their rear legs, their thick tails protruding. He was amazed at their hopping action and the length of each swerving leap.

He stepped out into the open to investigate what he took to be a depression at the centre of the clearing, perhaps a waterhole, where the animals appeared to have been drinking. He found nothing but further patches of oat grass and scrub.

As he turned to make his way back to the gulley entrance, he heard voices behind him and froze.

Two Indigenous tribesmen, one carrying three long spears across his shoulder and the other his water canister, were crossing towards him, conversing loudly enough to alert him to their arrival.

They were naked, their hair and beards wild. Sunil noticed that the warrior carrying the water wore a cape of red animal skin hanging down his back and across his shoulders, strung at the neck.

He could not read their expressions.

His first blinding reaction had him back on the Mannar beaches in Ceylon during the pearling season, when Indigenous Vedda tribesmen visited the pearl divers to sell their carvings and bows and arrows. Their moods were unpredictable and their appearances as fierce as the two confronting him.

Unable to restrain himself, he blurted a Tamil greeting. "*Vanakkam! Vanakkam!* Hello! Hello!"

He backed away as they approached.

They halted twenty metres away.

The warrior carrying the water canister placed it carefully on a patch of sand beside him.

He reached for a spear from his partner and held the shaft vertically, the glinting quartz barb downwards, barely touching the ground. "*Ngana nyinda?* Who are you?"

Sunil forced himself to remain expressionless despite the painful pounding of his heart. I sensed him wondering, *Is he asking who I am?*

The warrior seemed to deliberately avoid eye contact as he examined Sunil before calmly looking directly at him for several moments, then away.

Sunil took another backward step, alert to their every move, his heart still racing as the silent standoff extended.

A minute passed, then two.

The warriors continued to look him up and down. Then the first warrior extended his arm and rotated the spear to the horizontal, the barb facing Sunil and the shaft across the shoulder. He gestured across the grassland, sweeping the spear through a half-circle before pointing eastward, his frown now menacing. "*Wanthala nyindangu barraja? Gagarrala?* Where are you from, which country? To the east?"

Sunil, confused and alarmed by the aggression he saw in the swing of his spear, stood dumbfounded. *He must think I'm from another tribe, from inland*, he thought. *Perhaps an enemy.*

The warrior nodded, before pointing at his chest and flicking a forefinger at his companion. "*Ngatha Malgana. Ngathangura nhaganha barraja. Nayiwu nyinda nala yaninyina?* I am Malgana. This is my country. Why are you trespassing here?"

Fearing the worst, Sunil ducked, turned and sprinted for the shelter of the closest thickets. As he did so, he heard a warning shout and the rattle of spears. "*Hoh! Nyinda wujarnu matharra! Wirra! Wirra!* Hey! You, black stranger! Stop! Wait!"

Bent double and zigzagging desperately, Sunil heard the hoarse warning, before a second shout, fiercer than the first. "*Wirra! Gurra bajirri yana! Yugarri! Ngalingu nyindanha ngarrinmanha biladagurru!* Stop! Don't run! Stand still! Or we will spear you!"

In the menacing silence that followed, Sunil heard a final warning question ring out over his gasping breath as he sprinted on, "*Nyinda gulgathadi?* Are you deaf?"

Then, within several metres of the trees, a single spear whistled overhead, landed ahead of him and slid along the sand.

Bracing for the second to pierce his back, Sunil reached the grounded spear, picked it up and turned to face his attackers.

Shaking uncontrollably, his chest heaving, he held the spear horizontally in clenched fists, preparing to protect himself.

The warriors, who had loped after him, took up the same position in front of him, this time closer, and then, in a single movement, they swung their spears vertically once again, the barbs short of the ground.

The first of them gestured impatiently for Sunil to do the same.

Hesitant, he did so.

The first then grounded his spear, stepped forward and gestured to Sunil to do the same.

Suspicious that the other warrior had maintained his hold on his spear, Sunil waited.

The first again raised a hand and pointed at the ground, glaring as he expressed a disapproving hiss. This time Sunil reluctantly grounded his spear.

He saw a nod of approval and the flash of teeth when he stood and, though still fearful and distrustful, it struck him that he may have misread their intentions, despite the threat.

They had carried his canister of water, after all, and the

spear had missed him, though only narrowly. Besides, the other armed warrior now carried his spear casually across his shoulders once again, both his hands raised and relaxed across the shaft, observing developments.

"*Gurra icithayi, ngatha gurra bumanha nyindanha*, Don't worry, I will not hit you," the warrior said, his voice calm but firm as he stepped forward and, as Sunil flinched for a blow, he reached out with both hands and gripped Sunil by the left shoulder and right bicep.

He squeezed him as though to reassure him or show off his strength, before he placed Sunil's forearm against his own for a full half-minute, examining the dark skin texture and colour contrast of both.

Apparently satisfied, he stepped back and inspected Sunil from head to toe once again, puzzled. Then he reached up, ran a finger along Sunil's shaven jaw, and pointed at his groin. "*Nyinda wayabandi? Wurrinyu?* Are you a man or a woman?" he asked.

When he repeated the question and persisted in pointing at his groin, Sunil took off his shoes, undid the pewter buttons on his calico pants and removed them.

"I am a man, like you," he said.

Both warriors beamed before breaking into laughter.

"*T'i! Gutharra kuca warabadi! Nyinda ngugurnu wayabandi!* Yes! Two big balls! You are truly a man!" the second warrior exclaimed, pointing at Sunil's crotch.

His laughter subsided into a wide grin as he stepped forward and took Sunil's pants on the point of his spear. "*Nayi ngana! Nhanganha wurdbi thumanunyina manda galga wujarnugura!* Check this out! This is the skin that covers the stranger's backside and his legs!" he said.

He peered down at them, before reaching out to touch them suspiciously.

Then, gathering confidence, he dropped his spear and held the pants in both hands as he unfolded them, turned them inside out, checked the buttons and held them up to the sun as if to verify the weave.

Satisfied, he gave his partner a triumphant and cheerful shout, "*Nayi ngana!* Check this out!"

Amused, Sunil watched him sit down, stretch out a foot and insert it into the pants' leg. He stood and pulled the cloth to his thigh. Obviously wary of the feeling and watching nervously as his leg disappeared, he hopped comically around them before tearing them off, clearly so relieved to find his leg still intact that Sunil could not hold back a laugh.

Spurred on by Sunil's reaction and the ridicule of his partner, he inserted both feet and pulled the pants to his waist, struggling with the buttons before Sunil stepped forward to help him. "Here, this is how you do it," he said, relieved.

The pants were too large, and Sunil tightened the rope belt to hold them in place as the warrior, now highly stoked, leapt around them in a leg-stamping, arm-waving dance.

When he stopped, Sunil put his shoes back on and they made their way back to the water canister. "*Baba nyindaguru,* There's your water," the senior warrior said, pointing as they approached it.

As Sunil took it by the handle, the warrior pointed at the cloudless sky and shook his head. "*Bundu bardiyalu gurra bunduthayimanha marugudu.* There's been no rain and it won't rain tomorrow or for some time."

Then he sat and gestured for Sunil to join him.

When the three were comfortable, he pointed back at the water canister and then towards the east. "*Ngalingura maya bayirri yan, babamuthagurru. Ngatha ganmanha nyindanha babala barrangga.* Our camp is way over there. We have a plentiful supply of water. I will take you to the water there later."

Sunil shook his head and shrugged, both hands palmed up.

After pondering for several moments, the warrior said, "*Ngalingu nhanjanu wabagu warabadi wilithi gambanyu yuganga, garla gurrimutha. Nayi nhaga?* We saw the giant white sea-eagle yesterday. It caught fire, with lots of smoke. What was it?'

When Sunil shook his head again, he repeated the question, illustrating his description with exaggerated arm and hand actions representing a flying bird and gesturing skywards, coupled with explosive sounds, "*Nganharra nangiyanu nangguyanu yuganga marumaru!* Pockaa! Pock! Pock! Pock! We all saw it and heard it yesterday afternoon. The burning sea eagle."

"Ah, that was the kite," Sunil responded, demonstrating in turn as he spoke. "We set it on fire to signal the ships that passed us yesterday."

He knew that neither warrior understood word or gesture and realised they would have to return to the campsite for him to demonstrate. He pointed in that direction. "Come back to our camp. I can show you."

He stood and lifted the canister, again pointing west. "Come back with me. I can explain the kite. You can meet Gerrit."

The warriors jumped to their feet, shouldering their spears. The senior shook his head, again pointing inland. "*Mirda. Ngali yanmanha warrbathu ngurrala.* No. We'll both get back to our camp right away."

The other, beaming and still wearing the pants, told him, "*Marugudu nganharra nhanganha nyinda wilithi jinagabi ngurrala nyindangu.* Tomorrow we'll all come and see you and the white spirit at your camp."

Then he pointed at the late afternoon sun and slowly rotated his arm, first to the west, where he closed his fist, and then round to the east; and there, with the fingers and thumb of his right hand extended, he held his rising hand silhouetted against the sky above the treeline.

He held his position and gazed at Sunil with his eyebrows raised.

Sunil smiled and nodded. "You'll visit us at sunup tomorrow morning?" he asked, pointing westward.

"*T'i*, yes." the warrior said, "*i'i*," before bending to pick up his spear and joining his companion.

Sunil stood beside the water canister, watching them walk away.

They did not look back.

He slowly shook his head as they disappeared, relief rushing through him.

Barely able to believe what had happened, he pictured once again the explosive image of Gerrit's eye-catching kite signal flaring against the sky, his thoughts racing.

Gerrit won't believe this! I sensed him thinking. *His kite has brought us the best of good fortune in fact. Never mind the ships. Our rescue is coming from an unexpected direction. We will survive after all.*

At that moment I stepped towards the waiting waterfall with its vertical strings of light, and walked through it.

The bruhs won't believe it either. I thought, as I did so. *We've been waiting for the Malgana to make an appearance, but what a scene! An exploding kite and a Malgana warrior wearing Sunil's pants. Who'd've believed it? Certainly not Bones!*

But they did. They were hooked, wanting more.

It was the Aboriginal involvement, the Malgana warriors entering the scene that caught their imaginations, I think.

That, and the true story of the first Europeans and a Sri Lankan to settle, if you can call it that, on our continent.

Chapter 17

THREE WEEKS AFTER HIS first swimming lesson, Mozzie was the talk of Geraldton and Perth.

His science teacher, "Link" Baxter—we abbreviated "Link" from the "Missing Link", because he was so obsessed with the skulls of our ancestors from South and East Africa—took good care of him while they were away from school and in the spotlight.

Mozzie's face and his photos of the Greater Stick Rats' nests appeared in print in articles in the *Geraldton Guardian* and *Midwest Times*, the weekend *West Australian* and even the *Sydney Morning Herald*, as well as online in newsfeeds on their web pages. Let alone Facebook and some fans communicating with him on Instagram.

An essay appeared in *Wildlife Australia* a month later and even a by-line—we couldn't believe it until he showed us—in *Better Homes and Gardens*.

His brief, six-minute interview on the ABC's *Landline* was syndicated across channels Seven and Nine, appearing in shorter versions on their news channels one night.

Shy as he was, he handled it all well. Far better than we expected him to, to be honest. But we knew he was coming out of his shell as a member of the Alpha Bruhs, and that was great. We were his mates, and we shared in his success—at one remove, yes, for sure, but we shared it all the same.

Although his stardom only lasted a fortnight, his name and face were up in lights and we were thrilled for him.

So was some anonymous philanthropist who donated a mouth-watering $100,000 to the Harry Butler Institute at Murdoch University. He or she specified the donation was to be used to search for and protect Australia's endangered and extinct fauna, from the endangered Greater Stick Rat,

Numbat and Night Parrot among others—to the apparently extinct Desert Rat-kangaroos, Pig-footed Bandicoots and Crescent Nailtail Wallabies and the rest.

We googled Harry Butler, and wondered why the philanthropist selected him over the Steve Irwin's Wildlife Warriors. Willy Mack suggested it was because Steve's specialty was reptiles while Harry was a naturalist with a local reputation, because he'd worked on Barrow Island in the west. He'd studied the biodiversity there for years, and advised the Gorgon oil and gas developers whose project was threatening it.

At the same time, surprisingly, he or she rewarded Mozzie with a generous amount for his discovery, as I mentioned to you earlier. I have no idea how much it was, but he handed it all to Ruthie and she was so careful with it the family enjoying a better standard of living for the next six months.

That's loyalty for you, I thought. *Right there! One of our primary goals achieved by Mozzie, sharing his reward with his eight siblings and his dad. Looking after his family without a second thought. Thinking of others without complaining.*

We were truly proud of him.

And even prouder still for the challenge he faced up to next.

At the end of June one weekend, after his experience on the public stage, we were in the Lyons Den playing four-handed euchre in the late afternoon. We watched Spanner win the final trick, when Mozzie turned to Tiny and said, "I want to ask you for a favour, Tiny."

"No problem, Moz. What is it?"

"I want to check out the new Kalbarri Skywalk."

That caught our attention.

"*Jeeeesus*, Mozzie," Willie Mack said. "The *Skywalk? You?* Don't take this the wrong way, but aren't you tempting fate? Isn't that a walk on the wild side and a step too far?"

Mozzie gave him a cold stare, but said nothing.

"I don't mean to insult you," Willie Mack went on, his voice edgy, "but jumping a few metres into a pool with a soft landing at the Zuytdorp cliffs is way, way easier than walking twenty-five metres out along a steel mesh walkway, a hundred metres above the Murchison River. It only has a hip-high handrail preventing you from falling to your certain death."

"I know that," Mozzie said. "But you guys have done it."

"So?"

"So!" He shut down and gazed at Willie Mack with his mouth set.

Tiny put down his cards and collected the pack together. "*Now?*" he asked as he put the cards back in the box. "Willie Mack has a point, bruh. It won't be easy. You won't get vertigo, will you?"

"I don't know. Let's find out."

"We'll have to get moving, then," Tiny said. He looked at his watch. "Four fifteen. The gate closes around six. Anyone got fifteen bucks?"

"I'll pay," Mozzie said, livelier now. "I brought it with me. Ruthie gave it to me. She didn't ask what for."

"Just as well, I said. "She'd've had a fit, knowing her."

Half an hour later the Wrangler had taken us the forty kilometres to the Skywalk. We listened to South Summit on the way, joining in with the songs we knew the words to, but when we came to the last track, *Fallen Friend*, I was struck by such dread I bit my tongue and my insides twisted up so tight it took my breath away.

I didn't mention my experience to anyone when we got out and no one noticed how distracted and upset I felt.

We took the boardwalk to the second cantilevered walkway, so that we could look across at Nature's Window at the same time. There were four visitors, grey nomads by the looks, on the first one. We didn't want Mozzie distracted.

We were all nervous about what was coming next, and my gut was still tight with the frightening dread I'd experienced in the Wrangler.

As he had at the cliffs, Mozzie stopped several metres from the entrance to the structure.

He was pale and his hands were trembling like someone with palsy.

Bones had his arm around his shoulder. "Take your time, Mozzie," he said. "You've got all the time in the world."

"The rest of your life if it comes to that," Willie Mack agreed. "If it gets too difficult this time, there's no shame in putting it off and trying again."

Which was one sure way of egging him on, I noticed, as the muscles in Mozzie's jaw tightened and he gritted his teeth as if he was grinding them.

The rest of us formed a group beside him, line abreast and arms around our shoulders, as if we were part of his platoon about to attack a machine-gun nest in Viet Nam—*Viet Nam? Where did that come from? Dad's older brother Uncle Mark, of course,* I remembered, as we took three small steps forward. *He served there, at Nui Dat in 1972. As a volunteer, not a nasho whose marble had come up. Mum sometimes blames Uncle's cranky moods on Agent Orange and wonders if some of it rubbed off on Dad when he was a boy, twenty years younger than him. I sometimes wonder, too... But hey, if you're unsure of any of that, Google is standing by.*

Anyway.

It was repeat of the pool at the Zuytdorp cliffs, but not quite as painful for Mozzie and it didn't take as long.

"Grab the inside rail," Bones advised him when he made a move at last, "so you're looking inwards and not into outer space. And don't look down through the grating or your bum-hole will tighten up and you might feel sick. Don't do that until you're comfortable."

We lined up beside him as he clutched the rail with both hands and we shuffled sideways with him, slowly, taking one step and then another until he reached the end of the platform.

There he stopped, stared at the red gravel and the wattle trees he'd left behind for a full minute, took a mighty breath and released the rail to turn round and stagger three long steps to the outside handrail.

He gripped it tight, his knuckles showing white and his fingers red, as he buckled at the knees and ended up on his backside, looking out through the mesh panel of the protective fence.

We joined him, six of us in a row, looking out into space.

We sat there for a full ten minutes as Mozzie's rapid breathing slowed.

I had time to admire the western sky as it turned a blazing orange, the nearby cliffs and rocky banks of the Murchison River faded to dark bronze and stands of the early-flowering wattle trees below caught the dying light in brilliant shades of yellow.

Mozzie hadn't released the handrail. With a sudden loud grunt, he heaved himself upright. He deliberately looked around, pale but determined, and stared down through the grating at the silver ribbon of the river a hundred metres below.

Then he amazed us.

Still looking around, he arched his back and did a Ben, just without the teeth. He gathered a large gob of spit in his mouth, compressed his cheeks and spat as far as he could.

He watched it for the time it took to fall and disintegrate in the gulley wind below us.

We burst out laughing.

Then he released the rail and, without a word, strode back to the safety of solid ground down the middle of the walkway.

When he reached the gravel beside the boardwalk he turned to face us, smiling, tears shining on his cheeks, both hands up palm out as we passed him to the left and right, giving him high fives.

"Right on, Moz!" Tiny shouted. "Right on the money!"

Then he and Bones lifted Mozzie to their shoulders and carried him back to the Wrangler.

It was one of the most courageous acts I've ever seen.

And the tears?

Triumph and relief, in my book, the weird feeling I'd experienced in my gut leaving me wondering.

Chapter 18

THE NEXT TIME I set up the talismans and watched the images take shape, I discovered it was two hours after sunrise, at the clifftop campsite, in the morning after Sunil's meeting with the Malgana.

As the images crystallised, I saw a warrior appear from the nearest batch of trees.

He stepped out alone and unarmed, carrying three dead birds.

I recognised him at the same time as Sunil.

He was naked, except for the red hide cloak he'd worn before, tied at his throat and draped across a shoulder.

He strode into the camp and greeted Sunil, *"Nyinda ngugurnu?* Are you well?"

Sunil bounded to his feet. "Welcome," he said. "We were hoping you would come."

"Nyinda bulyarru? Are you hungry?" he asked, pointing at his open mouth and rubbing his stomach after placing two white- and grey-banded birds the size of chickens and a large, brown-feathered carcass the size of a turkey beside the fire. *"Nhanganha gutharra thanindi barduda. Guga gambaniya.* Here are two malleefowl and a bush turkey. You can cook the meat."

Ignoring Gerrit, who was sitting with his back to a Ti tree beneath the canvas strung across its branches and watching him closely, he turned to look down the cliff at the shipwreck.

Then he signalled towards the surrounding trees, calling others Gerrit hadn't noticed in the shadows and several men joined him, also unarmed. Their discussion was loud and cheerful, until one of them, stepping below the lip of the cliff to the platform, saw the carved wooden statuette of the Grecian sphinx ripped from between the gallery windows at the stern. It was propped against a rock halfway down, its yellow paint fading.

Gerrit watched him rear back, alarmed.

He sprinted back up the slope, calling out to the others and pointing.

They gathered around him staring in silence at the carving, before moving quickly back to the cover of the trees at the edge of the clearing.

As they faded back into the shadows, Gerrit assumed they were superstitious, and the statuette had spooked them.

How many others are concealed there? I sensed him wondering, the sound of several raised voices reaching him. *No one has so much as looked at me or acknowledged my presence.*

A short silence followed, and then he saw a tall old man emerge alone from the shadows. His thick, unruly hair was white and he was white-bearded and deeply wrinkled. His sharp, near-black, brown eyes were deep-set and hardly visible beneath a ridge of bony eyebrows and a sloping forehead. His nose was broad and the central membrane was pierced. Parallel body scars were ridged like a stairway up his belly and chest, much like Sunil. His back was rigidly straight, his face dignified.

His legs were bone and sinew, his stride long as he walked directly across to Gerrit, where he squatted at his level beneath the tree and looked him over. He avoided eye contact except occasionally, when his glance was piercing but calm, unemotional and full of authority.

He inspected Gerrit closely in silence, checked the weeping wounds and splints on his leg and showed surprise only when he saw the gin bottle half-filled with urine propped in the sand beside him.

He stared at it—and then, before Gerrit could stop him, he reached out his right hand and felt his crotch beneath his pants, releasing it at once.

Without a word, he stood and stepped to the other side of the tree trunk against which Gerrit was leaning. There he also sat, facing inland, his back turned on Gerrit. He looked directly ahead at the Ti tree scrub during a tense silence that lasted several minutes.

And then, in a baritone voice that shifted now and again into a high-pitched falsetto Gerrit could hardly hear, the old man began to sing.

His words sounded to Gerrit like a stream of musical notes rather than understandable speech.

The song lasted for ten minutes.

I felt Gerrit's nervousness grow into fear, and fear into terror as he thought it may be leading to his execution. He tried unsuccessfully to listen for cues from the tone and emotional pitch as to how he should react.

When the song ended, the old man was again silent for several minutes before he stood and resumed his position beside Gerrit.

For the first time, he smiled and pointed towards himself. *'Ngatha Kananggadi*, I am Kananggadi." he said. "*Kananggadi*," he repeated, emphasising it, then pointed at Gerrit, his eyebrows raised.

"I am Gerrit,' he replied. 'Gerrit de Waal."

The old man's smile widened. "*Gayirrit! Gayirri! Nyinda gayirri yanmanu. Nyinda Gayirrigayirrit.* Gerrit! From far away! You've come from far away. You are Gayirrigayirrit, Gerrit-from-afar."

He spread his arms wide, gesturing inland as though indicating the surrounding bush, trees and gulleys, confusing Gerrit even further. "*Nhanganha Gathaagudu, ngurra Malganangu uthudujadawana.* This is Gathaagudu, home to the Malgana people, our much-beloved country."

Then he nodded, as though assuming Gerrit had understood. "*Nyinda bardiyalu jinagabi wilithi, nyinda wiyabandi wilithi yanaangu gayirri wardandula.* You, you're not the white spirit of an ancestor returned from the dead, but a white man who has come from far to the west."

He nodded again, this time with more emphasis, before he added slowly and bluntly, "*Nyinda nyinamanha narla barrajala ngathangu. Yuganga, maragudu. Nyinda wiyabandi Malgana… Garimarangu.* You are welcome to stay here in my country from now on. You are a young Malgana man now, of Garimara descent."

Then he reached across and placed his right hand on Gerrit's left shoulder while patting his own with his left hand and repeated solemnly, "*Nyinda Malgana… ngatha Malgana. Nyinda Garimarangu.* You are Malgana… I am Malgana. You are of Garimaru descent."

He looked keenly at Gerrit as if expecting a reply.

"*Malgana?*" Gerrit tried. "*Garimarangu?*"

"*T'i*, yes," the old man beamed, before pointing at Sunil, seated at the edge of the cliff, observing them. "*Wiyabandi mathara bayirri, Malgana… Barungura.* The young black man over there, he is also now Malgana, of Barungu descent."

Then he waved his right hand and shouted at the trees, "*Nhurra nyarlu, gaba warrbuthu, matka atkajadi wanyu. Maruthayinyina.* You women, get over here quickly. Bring the Ti tree oil. It's getting late."

At his signal, two women stepped from the trees, one a teenage girl, the other older and carrying a hollow gourd of oil,

Gerrit was worried when the old man held out a hand and pointed at his wounds. "*Wirda wujarnugura marrigudu, mambu ardandanu marrithayiniyan.* The stranger's leg is injured. The bone is broken and has not set."

The two women knelt beside Gerrit, one on either side, and inspected the wound.

The older woman pointed at the urine bottle and whispered an instruction.

For a moment the girl looked fearful, before she gingerly reached out for the bottle.

She picked it up at last, scooped a hole in the sand two metres away and emptied it, before peering through the glass.

She seemed puzzled by its transparency.

She looked shyly over at Gerrit and tapped it with a fingernail *"Nayi nhanganhanu?* What is this?"

"It's glass. A glass bottle," he said, then repeated the word glass twice.

Her eyes lit up and she ducked her head before making her way down the cliff face.

Within minutes she was back with the bottle filled with seawater, and they began gently cleaning the wound with it.

Then, when the girl applied the oily ointment, Gerrit flinched and bit the inside of his mouth to offset the stinging pain.

The girl saw him wince. *"Nyinda warniyanu?* Did you fall?" she asked, her voice empathic, looking briefly up at him.

Captivated by her glance, Gerrit saw a change come over her.

Her shyness fell away as she spread the oil carefully across his wound, filling the air with the sharp scent of camphor.

When she was satisfied, she looked back up and, unexpectedly daring, reached out to touch the abalone shell necklace with what she thought was an albatross carved into it, hanging on a leather thong around his neck.

She pointed the albatross out to the other woman. *"Nayi naga nhanganha wilyara banduga.* Look at this albatross carved into the shell," she said.

My sea eagle! I thought. *Her albatross! Same image, but we have different totems.*

Glancing at Gerrit, she asked, *"Nayiwunga?* What's it for?"

She looked expectantly up at him, but he shook his head.

He had no idea what she'd asked him.

After a moment she tapped her breast as though making a connection that Gerrit couldn't grasp. *"Ngathangura banduga.* My totem is the albatross," she murmured.

Then she reached for the empty bottle and held it up.

"Glass," she said, before pointing again at the necklace pendant. She leant forward to touch the shell again and spoke the word, "Wilyara," then ran her forefinger across the albatross and repeated, "Banduga."

When Gerrit responded, "Shell… and albatross," and heard her correctly repeat the words, he was back in the Middelburg timber yards when he was a fourteen-year-old apprentice. There, an African carpenter from Angola, Serafino—an ex-slave—had told him that in losing your language, you lose your sense of self, but in sharing it, you experience the deepest sense of community.

Serafino was right, Gerrit thought.

At that moment he looked deep into the girl's dark brown eyes, and as she confidently held his gaze, he heard Serafino's laughter on a different occasion. '*Eé!* I am *ya makala mulat*, I am a black African, married to a blonde and blue-eyed Dutch beauty from Friesland—my perfect Severine! *Beto ke ebene mpi ivuari.* Together we are ebony and ivory, a perfect match.'

I saw Gerrit smile at the memory. *Ebony and ivory! Black and white! A perfect match!*

When the girl responded with a smile, he felt an unexpected glow of warmth and wondered what the future held in store.

At that moment the vision faded, quickly this time, leaving me back in my room after ducking through the waterfall of light.

I sat back on my bed, touched the pendant and wondered, as Gerrit had, what the future held—for me and Charlie Marks, that is.

If any.

But I was taking steps.

Cormac had set up a second easel with a medium canvas half a metre wide on it in his studio, with its spectacular view over the ocean. He'd shown me how to work with acrylics, and I'd laid my first blue brushstrokes across the canvas after studying my pastel of the wreck site Uncle Lennard had admired so much.

Do you want to know how I felt?

Liberated! And excited.

The future really meant something to me. Now that I was gunna mix the paints to produce unique colours that spoke to me, deep in my creative imagination. Now that I was gunna discover who I really was.

Cormac suggested *A Study in Blue* would be a good title for my first acrylic painting, the one we both knew would start my artistic career.

I decided to extend the title to *A Study in Blue for Charlie M* and hoped that it would give me a good excuse to talk to her.

It did.

Chapter 19

ONE EVENING IN EARLY August, I had chance to talk to Mozzie one on one, a month after he'd conquered his fear of heights on the Skywalk.

I'd been wanting to for some time.

We were in the Lyons Den and the others were outside looking for driftwood and firing up the barbecue.

"How's Ruthie and the mob?" I asked.

I wanted to find out how relations between him and his dad, Uncle Martin, had changed—for the better I was hoping—since all the publicity had gone down with his Greater Stick Rats discovery and after he'd given Ruthie his reward.

I had to work my way round to it.

"Good, with Ruthie," he said. "Really good. And good with the rest of the fam."

"So it's all good?"

"Yep."

"That's good."

"It is."

After a brief silence, which was normal for him but awkward for me, I came out with it.

"And Uncle Martin? How's he treating you now? Better?"

"Better? Better than what?"

"Is he at least *noticing* you, Mozzie? You know what I mean. Since your Mum died."

"Noticing me? He always has, not as much as Abe, Dave and Danny, that's all. I don't mind."

"Okay. Did you tell him about the skywalk?"

"No. Not yet. Maybe I will, maybe I won't. I don't have to. I know he'd be pleased if I told him, so I don't really need to. You guys saw me do it and I did it for myself. There is one thing he's done since then, though."

"What's that?"

"He took me out on *Buzz Off*. Just him and me. For the first time ever. Like I deserved it, or something. A special treat, and it wasn't my birthday."

"Wow. So how was it?"

"Great. We set some pots of Red Bluff and got a handful. And he let me steer. He told me he was letting me do that because he could see I was steering my life in the right direction, following the right star." He gave a brief, embarrassed chuckle. "I thought that was a bit much. He's never talked to me like that before."

"What's wrong with that, Mozzie? You sound embarrassed. Don't be. You should be proud of what you've achieved. So should he."

"Why? I'm keeping up with you guys, that's all. It's easy for you, that's the only difference. Now I'm catching up."

"You sure are."

A trip on Buzz Off*? I thought. It's enough, I guess. A special deal. Mozzie thinks the world of Uncle Martin. Loves him. That's clear from the way he talks about him. He's his dad after all, his hero, if you like. It's good to know Uncle Martin's starting to return that love, even if he's never put it into words. He lets* Buzz Off *do the talking, because his generation never used that sort of language or showed that sort of affection. Like my dad. But in his case always absent and disapproving. Or most of the time.*

I gazed at him as the smell of grilling fish mixed with lemon and frying tomatoes and chips drifted through to us, making my stomach rumble and enticing us both out to the barbecue.

"Half your luck, Mozzie," I said as we walked out, trying to keep my voice level. "Half your fricking luck. It's good to hear."

I didn't add "I wish my dad would do the same." It was on the tip of my tongue, but I thought better of it. I had Cormac's friendship after all. And Uncle Lennard's approval.

At that meeting we decided to walk from the wreck site to the Murchison River along the cliffs.

At night.

Under a full moon.

Never mind the Death Adders, Gwardars, Dugites and all.

"We need a real test," Tiny said. "A baptism of fire. And we need a ceremony to celebrate passing the test if we succeed. Like a passing out parade for 2024, you know what I mean? So we can call ourselves true warriors, true Bruhs of the Hexagonal Table from then on."

"Like a Masai warrior killing a male lion with his spear in the old days?" Mozzie asked, "And wearing its mane as a headdress to prove he's a man?"

He'd been reading one of Link's Anthropology books he'd lent him.

"Exactly, Moz. Right on." Tiny gazed around at us. "Any ideas."

We came up with a few, but the test that appealed was the one Bones eventually suggested.

"Listen," he said. "Summer's been spinning us yarns about the wreck of the *Zuytdorp*. His stories haven't been all that boring, which I didn't expect."

"Thanks Bones," I interrupted him. "Coming from you that's got to be a compliment."

"Yeah, well. In the last dream—"

"Vision," I corrected him.

"Vision, dream. All the same to me. Who cares where the stories come from, whether you're dead to it or awake? They come out the same when you're telling us." Then he grinned. "Just this side of sending us to sleep."

"*Jeeeesus*, Bones. Don't give us the shits, you pedantic dick. Spit it out," Willie Mack interrupted him. "What's the challenge?"

Bones pointed at me. "Who's the pedantic dick? Summer interrupted me."

"So, get on with it," Willie Mack said. "Summer's made his point."

"Okay. In the last episode Sunil and Gerrit were on the clifftop and were visited by the Malgana family, remember? The other survivors had taken off up north. Walking to Indonesia, apparently."

"To Shark Bay, Bones, where there were no cliffs," I corrected him again."

"Indonesia, Shark Bay, who cares? Because it left Gerrit and Sunil with a fricking problem. The Malgana family were on their way south to the Murchison, weren't they? And they weren't hanging around. Gerrit couldn't walk yet, and Sunil was diving and fishing to keep the two of them alive."

"So?" Tiny asked.

"So, when he *could* walk, what were they going to do? Sit there for the rest of their lives, with Sunny getting a Groundhog Day vison or dream—whichever—of their lives?"

He paused and took a long breath.

"Well?" Tiny asked.

"No, of course they won't hang around. They're going to make a run for it, south, to the Murchison. They would have been toey as. Carrying what water they've got left and either some dried fish or whatnot—"

"Hard-boiled seagulls' eggs and salted strips of Greater Stick Rats' jerky?" Willie Mack suggested.

"*Hey!*" Mozzie broke in but didn't continue.

"Maybe. Or Sunil's going to dive for their grub on the way."

"So?" Tiny asked. "Get to the point."

"Well, we do the same. If we succeed, we celebrate at Finlay's with fish and chips, oysters, squid rings and the lot.

A feast. Anything we want."

The idea was passed with a unanimous vote.

Then we got down to the fine details.

"We should walk it at night," Bones said, "under a full or three-quarter moon, like Sunil and Gerrit would have done. In their case to avoid the heat of the day, in ours for the challenge."

"At night?" Mozzie asked. "You sure?"

"Worried about the snakes, Mozzie?" Bones asked. "Why? You want to walk in the day so you can eyeball them before they eyeball you?"

"Something like that."

The vote for Bones's idea carried, considering the greater risk.

When Mozzie looked up the phases of the moon on our battered laptop, which Spanner had tuned into the Wi-Fi at old Ben Lyons's house, he confirmed the next full moon was Tuesday, 20 August.

"No good," Willie Mack said. "That's in the middle of term."

"The one after that's Wednesday, 18 September. School's out on the following Saturday. That'll be a waning moon, but it should give us enough light."

"Perfect," Bones said. "That's probably around the date Gerrit and Sunil would have started out too, with enough time for his leg to heal."

Then Mozzie worked on the map. "Sixty kilometres, twenty a night at two an hour for ten hours, including rests— three nights," he said, after a minute.

"Two k's an hour for ten hours? That's going some, Mozzie," Willie Mack said, "even if it sounds slow. Especially at night across country we've never seen… but it's meant to be an endurance test, so okay."

"The first night will tell," Tiny said. "We can adjust the pace if we have to."

"Maybe add an extra morning if we stop to fish," Spanner said.

"Stop to *fish*?" Bones said. "We're on a test here, not a fishing trip."

"Hang on, Bones," Spanner said. "If we get an early morning easterly, what's the harm in hanging out a balloon or two for Spanish mackas after the walk? We can put them on ice in Tiny's trailer and get Finlay's to cook us some macka steaks as part of the meal. My mouth's watering already."

Typical Spanner, I thought. *Saving dough again, eating our own fish. Good on him.*

Tiny was exempt, for starters. He'd be the referee and our safety officer, following us with the Wrangler and trailer. He'd take the tracks that led to the cliffs and set up camp, checking on our progress every so often on the two-way.

"What about sleep?" Mozzie asked.

"Good question, Moz." Tiny said. "I'll set up a tarp every afternoon ahead of you guys and you kip under it during the day on your foam mattresses. By Mozzie's calcs that's two nights of walking, two days of sleeping and after the third night of walking you keep going till you reach the river."

"Too easy," Willie Mack said. "Then we swim across and head for Finlay's, do we?"

"No, I'll get the tinnie and ferry you across, and if it's okay with Ruthie and Uncle Martin we kip at Mozzie's place. In Uncle Martin's new workshop. Should be okay on the concrete floor with the mattresses. Then we wander down to Finlay's in the evening and tuck in. Sound good?"

Uncle Martin had rebuilt his workshop. It took him three years. Cyclone Seroja got stuck in and flattened the original on 11 April, 2021, depositing its bits and pieces all over Kalbarri along with half the other buildings in the town. Some demolition job *that* was, way, way worse than an out-of-control wrecking ball with a mind of its own that couldn't give a shit.

We know.

We were there.

Ducking for cover when we were eleven.

Anyway.

"Sounds good to me." Bones said.

"Sure does," Spanner agreed.

"I can't wait" Mozzie said.

"What about lights?" I asked.

"The diving torch, for one—and we each have our iPhone lights if we need them." Willie Mack suggested.

"Okay, then," Tiny said as we did a communal high five. "We prime the two-way to keep in contact and we're set. That's the deal."

"Not forgetting a couple of helium balloons and a salted split-tail mullet or gardie bait or two, because *I am fishing* if the wind's right, doesn't matter what *you* blokes say," Spanner said. "This could be my one and only chance to fish off those cliffs after all."

He did fish.

Of course he did.

And he's never heard the end of it.

So, here's the thing.

It took us three nights, as Mozzie predicted.

We left the wreck site on the first night after a meal of 'roo steaks and jacket potatoes, after sunset,

The waning moon was rising over the western horizon, but wasn't high enough to show us the way yet. The night wasn't pitch black—we found ourselves in a sort of eerie half-light.

We began walking in single file across the heath, with Bones in the lead at first, carrying the two-way and using the diving torch to check things out when he needed to. We were carrying our iPhones for lights in case.

We agreed to share the lead between us, changing every two hours. That would give each of us the experience of being a leader, guiding and caring for those following us.

We'd thought about breaking the rule and carrying Tiny's Ruger .22 bolt-action Dugite repellent with us, but decided against it. We didn't have night vision glasses and things could go wrong if we took a pot-shot at a Dugite or a feral goat and it ricocheted and hit one of us.

Killed in action while on active service?

No thanks.

We did agree on a pair of snake protectors for the leader, though. Those behind him would take their chances in their runners. We were confident the vibration of the leader's footsteps would have any snake we came across hightailing it in the opposite direction.

Except that it was spring and the wind was cold, and a cold snake's going nowhere fast.

When we started out, I did shit myself once or twice, to be honest. My mouth went dry and I wished we'd all had the sense to wear them. A Death Adder hangs around, after all, hot or cold. It looks like a speckled brown turd and strikes across its coils with a thirty-centimetre reach, and at times in my imagination I was back in the snake pit with the Angolares whisperer among the Gabon Vipers.

The ground was rough at first, a mix of sand patches and poxy broken limestone. Regular steep-sided wattle-filled gullies running west to east were challenging and held us up as we scrambled down into them and up the other side, but later we found the heath along the clifftops covered in saltbush and samphire was easier going.

When the moon eventually reached its zenith and my eyes got used to the dark, I took in the luminous views, the ocean to our right the whole way occasionally lighting up in unexpected greens and dark blue streaks of moonlight.

The constant cold wind had us up and lively on the way, singing now then, cracking jokes and talking about our experiences over the last two years.

Willie Mack was in his element.

He had us laughing and groaning.

The cold must've reminded him of Scotland, and handing out blue beans in the dark wasn't easy.

You want an example or two?

Was that a yes?

Okay, here's the very first one he came out with.

"Hey Mozzie! You're not talking much tonight, but in this cold wind I can hear your teeth chattering."

After that he was on a roll.

It was like listening to Spanner yapping on about fishing, but more interesting. I didn't catch some of his riddles, though, when I was tuning in to the crash of breaking waves beside us. They were a constant soothing thunder.

And that fresh, salt-and-seaweed smell of the ocean all the way!

You can't beat it, I reckon.

Anyway, let's get back to Willie Mack.

"Hey, Bones! You want some sound advice? Give up singing!"

"Oi, Spanner! You're always worrying about your dough. What's the best way to make ends meet during the cost-of-living crisis? Become a double-jointed contortionist."

"Hey, Mozzie! You're a fan of Brian Cox. Ask him why we pass worms through our guts when we're alive and pass through the guts of worms when we're dead."

"Hey bruhs! Do you know that the electricity you don't pay for is free of charge?"

Three blue beans, delivered by Bones when the lead changed.

"Have I ever told you about the time I was a kid in Linlithgow Primary School and I had this ingrowing toenail? Yeah. They gave me the lead in the play that year. I was Pus in Boots."

You get the idea.

He's weird, but he lightened up the mood and the night passed quickly.

So quickly we were surprised by the pre-dawn light spreading in the eastern sky when we reached the camp Tiny had prepared for us.

We greeted him with a mix of relief—no snakes or feral goats—feeling dead tired, excited and proud of what we'd achieved together, as we settled down for breakfast. Tiny had brought the barbecue plate and already had the fire lit. We enjoyed two fried eggs, bacon, baked beans and a slice of toast and plum jam each, washed down with a tin mug of tea to fill our bellies, after the one muesli bar and litre of water we'd had during the night.

Then we settled in a row on our foam mattresses in the shade under the tarp strung across two Ti trees, and I was out to it at once, like someone switched out the lights.

Except for Bones and Spanner.

Bones had brought his treasured stopwatch with him. He was running the 800 and 1500 metres races for his age group in the Nationals in Brisbane next month and he had to maintain the work he was doing to peak on the right day. He measured out 150 metres of level ground and did the 12 sprints his dad had scheduled for him, even though he was dead tired after the night's walk.

Spanner, of course, went fishing. He spent an hour at it, after rigging up his rod with its seven hundred metres of 50 kilo line, three-metre wire trace, its four-ganged number nine-oh hooks with a triple at the end, its salted gardie bait with a frilled pink lure over its beak, its latex helium balloon and its metre-long PVC pipe rod holder—I know all this because I've heard it so often—but he didn't get a strike.

"The bloody easterly," he told us when we were preparing for the next night's walk. "It wasn't strong enough to get the balloon out." He tapped Bone's head with a forefinger. "Touch wood it'll be better tomorrow."

He copped three blue beans for that, delivered by Bones.

We found the going tougher during the second night.

It was rockier underfoot, and the gullies more frequent and deeper. The Ti trees and the wattle were denser too, their yellow flowers dusting the air and tickling the back of our throats.

You should've heard the coughing, swearing and spitting! Poor old Willie Mack sounded like an asthmatic almost bringing up his dinner. But he held it together and we responded to the challenge, maintaining the pace we'd set the night before.

Until I walked into a dozy mob of feral goats when I was in the lead.

They were snoozing in the shadows of trees at the bottom of the sixth gulley we had to cross. I smelt them at first, rank wet fir and hot piss, but before I had a chance to scream a warning and spotlight them with the torch they were all over us as they panicked and tore up the sides of the gulley.

I have no idea how many there were, but it was a fair-sized mob, considering the time it took for them to rush past us. We could hear the loud blowing of their warning calls as they clattered away into the darkness behind us.

Some of them were big.

Very big.

One hit me as it brushed past, sending me *manda* over *bibi*—or arse over tit in Australian—and badly winded on the rocks. The torch was smashed, bulb, reflector, protective glass and all when I dropped it, but I shielded the radio with both hands as I went down. In the same instinctive move, I turned on my side and ducked my head beneath my shoulder and upper arm to protect my face from the cloven hooves striking the rocks around me.

It was a heart-pounding twenty seconds.

The others scrambled down to see if I was okay.

None of them had been hit.

I tested the radio first thing when I sat up and was relieved to hear Tiny's voice crackle in reply a few moments later. When I apologised for waking him—it was one in the morning—and explained what had happened, he asked if the horns had got me.

After a quick check I reassured him they hadn't.

"A few grazes is all, Tiny," I told him. "Nothing serious. No one else was hit. We'll be using the iPhones for light from now on."

It took Willie Mack several minutes to pull the bits of broken glass from my elbow and behind my upper arm, with Bones shining his iPhone light on the wounds. Two handkerchiefs did the trick of binding them.

The rest of the night was uneventful, and we were as dead as we had been the morning before when we reached Tiny's camp.

"Groundhog Day!" Willie Mack said, when he saw Tiny's menu for breakfast. "Thanks Tiny. You're a life saver."

This time though, I didn't fall asleep at once.

I couldn't get in the zone. Maybe my encounter with the feral goats had stirred me up so much I still had a residue of adrenalin keeping me awake. Whatever it was, I watched Bones doing his sprints for a while, then wandered over to Spanner, who was sending out a balloon at the cliff edge.

Of course he was.

He unreeled the line as the balloon lifted in the easterly, flicking the gardie bait across the surface a hundred-and-fifty or so metres out, then he set the rod in the PVC rod holder he'd stuck in a crevice in the rock.

He gave me a broad smile as I walked over, forming a circle with the tip of his forefinger and his thumb. "Couldn't be better, Summer!" he shouted. "The easterly's in and it's the perfect morning for the mackas. Come on you little beauties! Breakfast is served!"

He'd hardly got the words out when a silver fish longer than your extended arms came up from below, attacked the bait and soared several metres into the air before crashing back below the surface.

The rod jerked over and the reel screamed out as Spanner gave a shout of triumph, "Yes! Go you good thing! Eeeeehah!"

He spent the next ten minutes leaning back with the rod bent double, its handle lodged in his solar plexus at first and then the crook of his arm, before easing forward and with four quick turns of the reel recovered some line, bent his back to lean back again, before easing forward for another four quick turns. When the fish gained the upper hand and went for a run, the taut line zipping in a half-circle you could see slicing through the water's surface, he adjusted the drag and let it run. Then, with another wild whoop, he resumed the battle.

Ten minutes later we could see the fish twenty metres out, on its side, close to the surface. It was tiring, but still had some fight left the closer it came to the rocks.

"What do you reckon, Summer?" Spanner shouted. "Is this the life, or what? He's a macka, alright! And a good one. Come on in, you little beauty. Come to Daddy."

Then he pointed at the long telescopic gaff lying beside him—he preferred that to the flying gaff others used.

"I'll let you do the honours, Summer."

He nodded down at the three shallow ledges below us. They led down like broad steps to deeper water where the surf was boiling as the rolling swells came in, higher waves sweeping across the upper ledges now and again.

"When I get him in close enough you put the hook into him, behind the gills."

I'd done it many times before in the tinny with a smaller gaff and smaller fish, never a pole that long in such turbulent water with a lively ten-kilo mackerel, if that's what it was.

I didn't say a word. I picked up the gaff, leaned out over the top ledge and held the hook above the waves rushing across the third ledge.

At that moment a three-metre brown shadow torpedoed through the water a metre down, took three-quarters of the fish into its mouth tail-first, and left the head with thirty centimetres of flesh and guts hanging on the line as it went slack and Spanner staggered back to regain his balance.

"You fucking bastard shark!" he shouted as he wound in the line. "Son of a bitch of a Bronze Whaler!"

Breakfast is served, I remember thinking. *Yes indeed.*

Spanner wasn't amused when I laughed and asked, "Behind the gills, Spanner?" as I gaffed the head for him, even though he'd lifted it clear of the water on the line.

The bite was a clean half circle.

Glad it wasn't me, I remember thinking.

Wouldn't you?

Spanner's shouts had woken Willie Mack, Bones had finished his sprinting session and Tiny left Mozzie asleep when they all came down to watch Spanner launch the balloon for the second time. He used a split-tail mullet rigged and sewn on for bait this time.

It took a little longer for the strike and the hook-up was less spectacular. There was a distant, short-lived explosive surface splash as the line screamed out, and so did Spanner.

The rod bent double and waggled wildly and the line was immediately taut and twanging, like it was about to break.

I won't bore you with a blow-by-blow rundown, though. It was the same sequence as before, except there was no shark this time and it wasn't a macka. It was a monster wahoo instead. Same family and same lean looks, with a different lateral line and longer jaw armed with teeth just as sharp. Two metres long and twenty kilos of streamlined silver muscle.

"It's got a bite like a white pointer," Spanner said, panting as he reefed it in and Bones steadied the gaff above the third ledge down. "We gotta keep the donger handy! Grab it, Willie!"

Willie Mack picked up the worn, sawn-off baseball bat lying on the rocks beside the holder.

That's when things went wrong.

Somehow the line got snagged, leaving the wahoo writhing in the boiling surf rushing across the third ledge down.

Spanner couldn't wind it in, and it was out of reach of Bones's gaff.

Before anyone could stop him, Spanner dropped the rod, leapt onto the first ledge, slipped on the wet rock of the second and was in the boiling water with the wahoo on the third as the wave receded.

He grabbed the line, pulled the fish towards him and as the next set came in and foaming water rose above his waist, he held the fish thumping madly across his chest. He had the thumb and fingers of his outstretched right hand through its gills, his left fist clamped around the shaft above its tail.

Trust me, Spanner put on the performance of his life.

We four have got it on video on our iPhone cameras.

The next wave knocked him to his knees, but he struggled with the fish up the incline to the second ledge. There he worked himself upright, and then, like a superhuman hammer thrower on anabolic steroids, he grabbed the fish by the tail with both hands, swung it sideways and hurled it across the top ledge onto the rocks beside us where it flopped around, before stiffening and shivering as if it had palsy.

We were laughing at Spanner fit to bust, even though it was so dangerous for him.

How he didn't drown, get bitten or hooked on one of his nine-ohs I have no idea.

But he didn't.

Willie Mack handed him the donger; Spanner did the rest and Tiny put it on ice in the esky—with its tail hanging out beneath the lid.

On the last night we descended the cliffs for the first time. We climbed down to a series of sandy coves between rocky ridges and platforms. We could vaguely see them in the moonlight, running out to inshore reefs boiling with surf.

Eventually the cliffs petered out and for the last few kilometres as dawn was breaking, we found ourselves walking in the soft sand of a sloping beach curving away towards the river mouth.

We turned upriver just before eight, Kalbarri Township waking on the opposite bank, the only signs of life the tiny figures of half a dozen surfies with their helmets on riding the runs of breakers beside the towering Red Bluff.

Tiny was there to greet us, sitting on the foredeck of the tinny in the shallows.

"So, how'd you go?" he asked Bones when the greetings were over and he'd handed us each an icy Coke.

"Brilliant," Bones said. "Just brilliant."

"And your impressions, Willie? Bit different from Scotland?"

Willie Mack paused, and then, "Two words for it. Rugged… but bloody beautiful, even at night."

"Rugged but bloody beautiful? That's four."

"Four then, but I'm not sure Sunil and Gerrit would've been so complimentary."

"He would if he'd had a fill of the fish and chips Ruthie's about to feed you."

"*Not my wahoo?*" Spanner butted in. "*Surely?*"

Concern and flight or fight were written all over him.

"Yep. The very same."

"*Bugger*! I told you I wanted to give it to Finlay's for a feed."

"Relax, Spanner. Finlay's got the other half."

"That's alright then."

And it was alright, that evening.

More than alright.

It was a feast to die for, under the old eucalypt tree and the orange bougainvilleas, outdoors, in Finlay's Garden restaurant. We had live music too, as if it had been laid on for us on that special evening. Two older bloke guitarists singing Country and Blues, turn-and-turnabout. Not quite South Summit or Elvis, but "Beggars can't be choosers," Willie Mack said.

When Tiny was ordering for us, I thought of Sunil and Gerrit enjoying a beer beside the dunes in Zeeland before they took to the sandyachts, the salty sea smell reaching them on the afternoon wind.

Same sea smell here, just a different drink. And menu, if they'd ordered a meal.

Want me to tempt you?

Make your mouth water?

It did ours.

We decided we'd all order the same. It was our second anniversary as Alpha Bruhs of the Hexagonal Table, after all. We'd been together for two years now, as mates, without too many disagreements, and the curtain was soon coming down on 2024.

For starters, whole Exmouth tiger prawns and squid rings served with Finlay's special cocktail sauce.

For mains, beer battered Kalbarri wahoo fillets—caught by Spanner—with chips, Caesar salad, and Finlay's unique tartare sauce... second helpings all round.

For sweets, chocolate mousse with berries and ice cream.

Yum.

All washed down with a Coke at the restaurant, and a can of Rocky Ridge Draught waiting for us on ice as a special one-off treat at the Lyons Den before we headed home.

Before we stood to leave, Bones dug into his pocket and handed me his stopwatch.

"You're the psychic," he said. "If your coin works for you, this might too."

I knew what he was after and immediately had my doubts. *Me and Tyler Henry on the same song sheet? No way.*

The others were watching and the guitarist was going for it. *Islands in the Stream* if I remember rightly.

"I've haven't tried it with a different talisman and never on someone else, Bones," I said, sensing all eyes on me. "Least of all in public. But okay, why not? I'll give it a go. What do you want to know?"

"Easy. Am I going to win the 800 and the 1500 next month?"

I held the stopwatch in both hands, closed my eyes and concentrated, shutting out the noise.

Nothing at first, and then it was very different from the start to a vision of the ship. It was like a faint mist was clearing on a cinemascope screen and I saw a running track at the same time as I didn't see it, if you get my meaning. I saw it through a glass darkly, as Twiga once mentioned the saying goes.

It was insane, unexpected and mysterious.

Very weird, in fact.

A track with runners on it. See through runners, transparent figures wearing their state colours, all going for it.

It was a two-lap race, and Bones? I saw him staggering down the home straight, clutching his side with a stitch, finishing in fourth position behind two Victorians and a Queenslander.

And the 1500 metres?

Ah, that was more like it.

I saw Bones and the Victorian who won the 800, sprinting

neck and neck around the final bend, when Bones did a John Landy and looked to the left, the wrong way. The Victorian did a Roger Bannister—do you remember that? No? Check it out on youtube. 1954, at the Vancouver Empire Games. It's a classic—and passed him on the outside to win the race.

I handed him back the stopwatch.

Second and fourth!

How could I tell him that? I couldn't hex him in advance. Give him the bad news. Put the idea of losing in his head.

Uncle Lennard was right. I recalled his words. *You might see something you don't want to report. What do you do then?*

"So, what did you see," Bones asked, itching for an answer. "Anything?"

Before I could tell him it hadn't worked and I'd seen nothing at all, my mouth did a Bones and sounded off thoughtlessly by itself, which was ironic.

"Yeah, nah, bruh. I saw you win both races, no questions asked. That's what I saw. You even had this stitch in the 800 but it didn't stop you. You put those Eastern Staters to the sword."

To the sword? Thanks, Twiga.

You can imagine what he said when he got back the following month after the Nationals.

"You and your fricking psychic abilities, you cappin *bullshit* artist, Summer! Your prediction made me overconfident. I would have won both races otherwise. That's the last time I listen to you, you dumb arsed shit for brains."

I was stoked. *The sceptic's back!* I thought. *It's great to know you're mentally tough once again, Bones!*

I lifted my eyebrows, shrugged my shoulders and gave him a fake apologetic smile. "I did warn you, Bones. I'd never done it with a different talisman for someone else. No wonder it didn't work. I made you overconfident. I must've been reading your mind."

"Smartarse!"

And that was the last time I tried a different talisman on someone else, to be honest.

To this day.

When I handed the other talismans back to Uncle Lennard, I found it hard parting with the sea eagle. When I lifted it to my lips and said goodbye, I felt a pain in my chest, like someone in there with a sledgehammer was breaking out.

My personal totem, I'd become attached to it.

I could hear my dad saying: *You're a sentimental drongo, Sonny! Get over it. Who needs a lucky charm? Grow up and become a man, like your brother.*

Chapter 20

Okay.

Now then.

Poor Mozzie.

The strangest story of them all.

Like I mentioned at the start, it happened on 4 January, 2025, three days after my fifteenth birthday.

A surfie found his abandoned plastic yellow kayak floating out to sea from the Murchison river-mouth, with three crab nets on board and a dozen Blue Mannas in a red bucket trying to escape. He paddled it in and handed it to the Police, exactly an hour after a Japanese tourist on the Skywalk thirty-seven kilometres away spotted Mozzie's naked body on the rocky riverbank 100 metres below.

Mozzie had been crabbing alone for Ruthie the evening before, and never came home.

So how did he make it from crabbing at nightfall opposite the Jetty Seafood Shack in Kalbarri, to lying dead below the Skywalk overnight?

He couldn't have walked it solo, not that far. We knew he didn't get a lift and jump, not in a million years—although the Police considered that possibility. They even put out a request to anyone who may have seen him hitch-hiking along the Ajana-Kalbarri Road, or the road beyond the turnoff to the Skywalk.

No way. Not Mozzie.

Someone had murdered him.

And insulted him by removing his clothes, perhaps to avoid the possibility of DNA evidence. The search party sent out to look for his clothes on horseback, found nothing.

The question us five bruhs and everyone else was asking once the shocking news got out, was who and why?

And what do we do about it?

Up till now I've hinted to you that Geraldton is Australia's illegal drugs importing gateway in the west. Remember Tiny's comment about drugs at our first meeting in the Lyons Den? And Cormac's painting of the *Man in a Pink Shirt*?

This long, wild stretch of mostly empty coast is difficult for Australia's Border Force—the ABF—to police, and the bosses of Australia's drug syndicates lick their lips and count the dollars as they smuggle it in.

Cashing in, sometimes by the billion.

Over recent years you have seen the news reports of huge hauls that have been seized with the help of international law enforcement agencies. What you don't see until they hit the streets are the mouth-watering amounts that get through.

You don't believe me? Because I'm sounding like a fricking know-it-all journo?

Sorry, but it's true.

I've heard it talked about since I was a kid. It's common knowledge.

Anyway, back to Mozzie.

What we didn't know until a day later, was that after a year-long international investigation, the ABF had been tipped off that a quarter tonne of meth was on its way to Australia aboard the container ship *Jerung Emas*. She was sailing out of Port Klang in Malaysia to Fremantle and an eastern states syndicate was going to pick it up, offshore, between Kalbarri and Geraldton, when she passed by at night on 2 January.

The ABF weren't sure how the syndicate intended to recover it, so they laid an ambush.

They sent in plain-clothed officers to look like tourists and establish lookouts at convenient points along the coast from Dongara and as far north as Shark Bay. How many? Your guess is as good as mine. And they investigated all the trailered boats that had come into the area in the last month.

Enter Uncle Martin aboard *Buzz Off.*

Crayfishermen in Geraldton and Kalbarri were stoked with the news that the ban on the export of crays to China had been lifted, and the trade would kick off again after 31 December, 2024.

So, on New Year's Day, Uncle Martin went out with Dave and Danny to catch their first batch of reds and whites for export. The next morning they were out before dawn as usual, when Dave spotted a flickering red light snagged among their cray-pot buoys.

When they pulled up alongside, they found a small black island of twenty plastic-wrapped floating parcels tied together, with a red beacon going for it in the centre.

It took them an hour to separate the parcels, load them on board and find out they'd discovered a hefty drug haul, packed in foam-lined eskies. The flashing light was a faulty personal locator beacon, its battery running low.

The *Buzz Off* was a kilometre and a half offshore, at sunrise, in full view of anyone on the cliffs with binoculars.

Shocked, and concerned he'd been seen, Uncle Martin radioed the Fishermen's Cooperative in Geraldton to let them know he was coming in. He made it sound as if he was intending to offload his catch, in case anyone was tuning in.

Meanwhile Dave and Danny stacked the parcels below, out of sight.

Then Uncle Martin turned *Buzz Off* for Geraldton and revved up to cruising speed, the twin hulls of the Shark Cat leaping from one wave crest to the next in spite of the extra weight of its illegal cargo, a two-metre rooster tail of white foam spraying out the back.

Five hours later, when Uncle Martin pulled in alongside the wharf at the Fishermen's Co-op, six plain clothed AFP officers were there to meet him. They swarmed all over the boat, found the drugs, and held Uncle Martin, Dave and

Danny in the cabin. After thirty minutes of confused grilling, Uncle Martin convinced them he'd come across the drugs by chance and wasn't involved.

That complicated things.

News of the haul hadn't filtered out, so the ABF officers decided to leave it on board, to entice whoever was in the area to pick it up to come looking for it. Assuming, of course, that they'd also seen Uncle Martin offshore at Red Bluff.

What they didn't bank on was the workers in the Co-op, who witnessed the activities aboard the boat, talking about it. Clearly something big was going down and the plain clothes' camouflage of the ABF officers wasn't fooling anybody.

That evening Uncle Martin Buzzacott was the talk of the town.

Geraldton's that sort of place.

"Leaky as an old bloke's waterworks when his prostate's playing up," Willie Mack said, when we heard the rumours.

Anyway, no one suspicious turned up that day or the next.

By 4 January, our favourite youngest bruh, Mozzie, was dead, and his dad and two older brothers were still in Geraldton, assisting with the investigation.

That's when the full extent of the drug haul was released to the airways and across the internet.

Another win for the good guys, but not for Uncle Martin. He spent an hour with Forensics in Geraldton identifying Mozzie's mangled body, when it was brought in by the RAC Rescue chopper sent up from Perth.

At our next meeting in the Lyons Den we were stunned and filled with grief, horrified and wild with anger. Our world that had seemed so secure and welcoming had been personally invaded and all that we believed in turned upside down. Our band of bruhs had been suddenly and shockingly violated. One of us was dead, and each of us felt a part of us had died with him.

I couldn't speak at first, fighting not to cry—which Bones did openly as the sobs tore through him every now and again. Spanner was working that day at the Garnet Mine and Willie Mack was very pale and withdrawn, which is difficult for him with his freckles and his usually talkative tongue.

Tiny was quiet and not as forceful as he usually was.

He was deep in thought.

That means trouble, I remember thinking.

I was wearing the birthday present Bones had surprised me with—an abalone shell pendant on a leather thong with a sea eagle carved from another shell glued to it.

"I know how upset you were when you had to give the other pendant back to your Uncle Lennard," he said simply. "I thought you might like this. Maybe it'll work like the other talisman and you can give us the next *Zuytdorp* episode."

It turned out he'd convinced his parents to camp at the Greenough River mouth overnight so that on Saturday, 14 December, 2024, he could dive for abalone during the one hour of the licence period that morning.

"Three shells were enough," he told me. "That's all I took. We don't eat them. Julie May, my friend at Marlon Craker's Jewellers, did the rest. It rocks, doesn't it?"

I was lost for words. *Bones giving me a birthday present? And exactly what I wanted? Did he read* my *mind this time, or what? Unheard of!*

"It more than rocks, Bones," I said, as I put the pendant to my lips before hanging it round my neck and embarrassing him with a hug. "It's *fire*, bruh. It's fricking *lit*. Thank you! Thank you! Thank you!"

Anyway, it was Tiny who spoke at last when we'd settled.

"Look here, bruhs," he said, "I know we're hurting, and hurting bad. It's like we've shared whatever Mozzie had to go through because we've imagined it and taken the fall with him. But we have to look this situation in the eye. We must become men and fix the bastards up who did this, one way or the other. Because they did it to *us*, as well as him. I can hear him whispering to me right now, "Way to go, Tiny." Can't you? He *is* one of us, not *was*, and always will be."

Which is probably as long and as passionately as I have ever heard Tiny speak.

"So what do we do?" Willie Mack asked. "What *can* we do? Where do we start?"

"Here's the thing, whoever did this must have seen Uncle Martin pick up the meth—from Mushroom Gorge or Rainbow Alley," Tiny said.

"Or Red Bluff," Bones suggested.

"Yep. Or Red Bluff. But what I want to know is, how did he know it was Uncle Martin's boat… and Mozzie was Uncle Martin's kid? They must have been eyeballing Kalbarri for some time. Watching everyone's movements and minding everyone else's business."

"Or there was a local involved," Willie Mack said.

"Maybe more than one. Who knows? The question now is what will they do next? They've lost a quarter of a billion bucks. That's not peanuts. They must've outlaid a fortune for it, if that's the way it works. They're going to take revenge." Tiny said. "They already have, starting with Mozzie."

"What, kill the rest of the family?" I said. "You're kidding. They've spilt enough blood already."

"I'm thinking more destroy Uncle Martin's business so he can't make a living. Burn *Buzz Off*, for starters. Set fire to his house and workshop. Especially if they aren't insured. We know how hard up they've been," Tiny said.

"So where do we come in?" Bones asked. "Become five mercenaries, armed with your bolt action .22 and take them on once we know who they are?"

Tiny gave him a quiet smile. "Something like that, Bones. I've been giving it some thought. If I was in their shoes I'd pick an easy target first up, like they did with Mozzie. I'm thinking *Buzz Off*. She was used to transport the drugs. They can't get to her while she's still under guard in custody in Geraldton, but when she's back in Kalbarri in her berth at the jetty she'll be easy meat. A few cans of fuel are all it'd take."

"So?" Bones asked.

"So we talk to Uncle Martin when he gets back. We stay at his place, sleeping in the workshop like we did after the walk. We take turns watching *Buzz Off* at the jetty from the workshop roof at night. It's flat, and even though it's corrugated iron we can make it comfortable. We tee up half a dozen of Uncle Martin's trusted friends in Kalbarri and let the ABF and Police know what we're doing. One phone call and whoever they are is fried. That way we're also there if they try on something at the house."

"How long for?" Willie Mack asked. "I'll have to convince my folks."

"Me too," Bones said.

I knew Mum and Dad would be okay with it. Becoming a man. Taking up my social responsibilities. Having a mate's back. Filling Billy's shoes, the ones he grew out of when he was fifteen and scoring straight A's.

"First term starts on Wednesday, 5 February," Tiny said. "If nothing happens up to a week before that, it's probably not going to happen. They've gone back to where they came from. Slipped through the ABF net."

But it did happen.

On Wednesday morning, 22 January, when Tiny was on watch, with Bones asleep beside him on the roof because it was cooler up there. At 2.30 am.

Three shadows, a jerry can each, appeared from nowhere— they must have driven into Kalbarri earlier that night and parked up the waterfront out of Tiny's view—walking like they didn't have a care in the world along the jetty to *Buzz Off*, in the third pen from the end.

Within three minutes of Tiny's call, six cars converged on the jetty. The spotlights on two utes blinded a short, broad-shouldered older bloke with a bikie's hair and beard and two younger blokes, who looked to be in their mid-twenties. One of the younger ones was already aboard and the other was handing up the third jerry can. They were caught frozen in mid-act, one leaning over the side and reaching out his right arm, the other with the can at shoulder height.

Two shots fired over their heads was all it took—'roo shooter Tim Halloran's Highlander M85 bolt action .223 did the business and woke up half of Kalbarri into the bargain.

Turns out they're known crims from Sydney and still in custody now. We're waiting for the charges to be declared and laid. Proving they murdered Mozzie won't be easy, if at all possible, to be honest—but we five Alpha Bruhs of the Hexagonal Table have taken a big step towards clearing the ledger for him, with the help of his dad and five close friends. It felt good when they congratulated us, like we'd cooperated with a group of men who understood where we were coming from and were proud of all we'd done.

Vale Mozzie Buzzacott, our bruh and our good friend.

You would have been proud of us too, I remember thinking, *but I have a sneaky feeling you were there with us, leading the charge with the gloves off.*

The following day we were at the Lyons Den, when old Ben and Bazza called in.

"What are you boys doing for a memorial at the place Mozzie was found?" he asked. "I think you should do something to make sure he's remembered."

"You mean like a wooden cross with flowers on the side of the road when someone ploughs into a tree?" Spanner asked. "That always gives me the creeps, to be honest."

"That's the idea. That way he's not forgotten."

After some discussion, Willie Mack came up with the answer we agreed to.

"We like the sign you gave us for the Lyons Den, Ben. That rocks. How's about we do something similar, with an epitaph burned on it with your welding flame?"

"Sounds good to me," Ben agreed. "What epitaph, though?"

Willie Mack responded without a second thought. "Tiny's given us the epitaph. I took it down when I heard him say it. I haven't forgotten it."

"*Me?*" Tiny said. "You taking my name in vain again, Willie? What have I said this time?"

Willie Mack pulled out his notebook and flicked through the pages.

"Here it is… He *is* one of us, not *was*, and always will be."

Ben clamped his lips together and drew his mouth down at the corners thoughtfully, as he nodded yes. "Sounds good," he said. "The rest of you okay with it?"

"No worries."

"Go for it."

"Good one."

"Right on the money."

By his expression I guessed old Ben was picturing himself already firing up his oxy flame and burning it into a Jarrah plank.

And so it was, though Ben added a touch of his own to the epitaph.

It wasn't a cross, as such, but a sanded and then lacquered metre-wide plank of Jarrah with two metal spikes attached, so we could hammer it into the ground.

Mozzie Buzzacott (14) was burned on it, and below the name in smaller print, *He is, not was, and always will be one of us six Alpha Bruhs of the Hexagonal Table.*

The epitaph took up two lines.

The day before we went back to school, Bones, Tiny and I climbed down the cliff face to hammer it in.

Bones left Mozzie's green ribbon and silver swimming medallion dangling from it.

I have no doubt it's still there to this day.

Chapter 21

O N Sunday, three days before the citizens' arrest, Uncle Martin and Ruthie held Mozzie's funeral at Lucky Bay.

His funeral? I mean his memorial service, a celebration of his life.

Ruthie involved us five bruhs in the decision to sprinkle his ashes in the lagoon behind the Lyons Den, where he'd spent so much time perfecting his swimming skills. We chose a spot not far from the camping site, so that anyone who wanted to attend could park.

Uncle Martin had arranged a cremation in Perth for Mozzie's body, when Forensics released it there. He was coming back with his ashes.

"We have to get Uncle Martin to put this in the coffin with him before he's cremated," Bones suggested, when we were discussing it the day before Uncle Martin left for Perth. "I meant to give it to Mozzie before he died."

He handed Ruthie South Summit's new album *Bliss*, in its cherry-red cover.

"I managed to get him one of the last copies before they ran out."

"Right on the money, Bones," Tiny agreed. "He's going to need some music where he's going. What better than his favourite group?"

"What sort of birds are these? Brolgas?" Ruthie asked, looking at the curving line of five black stork-like birds on the cover, wings spread and flying over the title.

"I can hear Mozzie correcting you right there, Ruthie," Willie Mack said, with a smile. ""What *are* you, Ruthie?" he'd say. "They're five Great Egrets. Don't you know that?""

"He'd be the one to get it right," she said.

He sure would, I thought. *And five Great Egrets? That's got to*

I reached for the album and checked the list of songs. A rush of relief flooded through me when I saw that *Fallen Friend* was not listed, though the first band was *Take Me Down* and the last *We Are the Lions*. Somehow South Summit had got it right again, when you think about it.

That morning a light easterly was in and we had an outgoing tide, the circle of ashes floating out into the deeper ocean in a Viking farewell without the flames.

Ruthie had picked two baskets of golden Mooja Christmas tree flowers from the two trees blooming in their garden at the time.

I'd admired them when we were mounting guard over *Buzz Off*. The rich gold cascade of flowers covering them held me captive each time I looked… and I remember thinking *A Study in Yellow* for my next painting. Very Vincent Van Gogh, with his wheat fields and sunflowers. No? Google's there for you with AI if you need it, as I've often mentioned before.

Ruthie handed a bunch to everyone who attended.

There were at least a hundred of us there.

The school arranged a bus and many of our kids came, including Charlie M, to my surprise. I hadn't seen her for a while, and a burst of shock ran through me like electricity as it always did, when I saw her disembark. You know the feeling—when you find yourself out of breath before you regain your senses.

Anyway, there we all were, in a line, wading out barefoot on the sand with the water to our knees, holding our yellow Mooja flowers.

After Ruthie's speech—she took over from Uncle Martin when he broke down—Uncle Martin tipped the ashes out, and we threw the Mooja flowers towards him as the ashes spread like a patch of oil on water without the rainbow effect.

The scene was beautiful, like in a dream. A rich yellow

carpet bobbing around his ashes as they floated slowly out to sea.

Mozzie would have loved it if he'd been there. Perhaps he was.

I said the effect was beautiful, but what happened to me next was even more so.

I was watching the gold and grey raft float slowly out, when someone surprised me by taking my right hand in theirs.

I looked around and almost died, as they say.

Charlie M!

I hadn't seen her coming, but she'd worked her way towards me and slipped her left hand into my right.

What a moment!

I will never forget it.

The burning rush of adrenalin so strong it took my breath away.

The tears that filled my eyes without running down my cheeks.

My heart racing in my chest like Bones sprinting down the home straight in his next 800.

"Hi, Summer," she said, the smile in her lit green eyes catching me off guard and not hiding the fact that she was crying.

"Charlie," I managed in a whisper, as my mind screamed, At last! At last! At last! At last!

I gripped her hand as if I'd never let it go, which I never will, then eased it in case I was hurting her.

"It's alright," she said, responding by tightening hers. "I won't break.

That's all we said for several minutes, as we both looked out at the horizon.

That's all we needed to say.

Until an hour later, when we were in Cormac's studio and he'd left us alone.

I'd told her about the *Study in Blue* without mentioning *For Charlie M*, and convinced her to give the bus a miss and come with me, Spanner and Cormac back to their place to see it.

It was still on the easel, dried and cured.

I took it and held it out to her.

She walked to the open window and held it up so that the range of blues were backgrounded by the ocean and the sky.

That's when she read the full title.

I heard her gasp and saw her sob, her eyes glistening as she looked round at me.

"I love it, Summer. It's beautiful"

She walked across the studio, and holding the painting between us, she leaned across and kissed me.

It was my first kiss ever, and I've never forgotten it.

Nor have I forgotten the second, when Charlie put the painting back on the easel.

She took a Mooja flower she'd saved from her pocket, held it tight and whispered a soft "Thank you," before closing her eyes and leaning in for another kiss.

Acknowledgements

THIS NOVEL WOULDN'T HAVE seen the light of day in its current form without the cooperation and advice of others. This is the second time I've made the leap into YA writing and I was floundering without them. I owe them my deepest thanks.

My perceptive seventeen-year-old granddaughter Kaylee Monaco to start with. She surprised me with the depth and accuracy of her know-how and her enthusiasm. She guided me in aspects of the YA novel writing process I had little clue about. Thank you Kaylee, for your patience and invaluable advice.

Lynne Stringer, my reliable and brilliant editor who has devoted so much time to correcting and tweaking all my work over the years. Lynne's changes are always spot on. They never fail to improve the word choice, plot sequences and storylines. I owe you my heartfelt thanks.

Tireless James Munro of Australian e-book publishing, whose extensive technical skills I have tested many times. Thank you for your creativity in preparing my work for publication to the highest standards and for your persistence and timeliness.

My special thanks to Ben Bellottie, senior Malgana Aboriginal man, Shire Councillor and Chair Person of the Yadgalah Aboriginal Corporation in Denham, Shark Bay, for permission to use the Malgana language in portraying a Malgana family in 1712. Further thanks also to the Yamaji Language Centre in Geraldton for their 2003 book on the Malgana language: *Malgana Wangganyina*. It was an invaluable reference.

Many thanks also to my pre-publication researchers, readers and advisers whose guidance and interest I value: Mike and Jenny Purchase, Karen and Elly Monaco, Gill Bennett, De Kropach, Bruce and Inka Hutton, Cam and Jae, Jessica Lee, Dayna Norris and Kay Stehn. Without you none of my work would have reached the reading public.

About the Author

B ORN IN TANZANIA, FROM the age of six I was fortunate to grow up in Mombasa on the Kenya coast. One of my goals in life was to research the Arab, Chinese, Portuguese and Dutch explorers who sailed along the East African Swahili coast for centuries.

I migrated to Perth, Western Australia, in 1963. After a 7-year stint as a High School teacher, I transferred to Human Resources and worked on remote mine sites in the Pilbara, Northern Territory and Papua New Guinea. This brought me into close contact with local Indigenous people. I found their culture, deep rooted love of country, resilience and unfailing sense of humour inspirational.

I retired in 2008 and since then have dedicated myself to writing fictional novels based on historical themes. 3 of these comprise the Truth and Reconciliation Trilogy: *Bright Flame Dark Shadows* and *The Kite Flyer* and *Alicia*. They draw on 20 years of archival research undertaken in Australia and the Netherlands (Zeeland), and an appreciation of Australia's First Nations people, who have survived the effects of European settlement and colonialism. The trilogy gives you a fresh look at Australia's colonial history and reflects the current dialogue between the Aboriginal First Nation people and the rest of Australia.

I have also written two YA novels, *The Dreams of Summer Dartson* you've just read, and *My Brother, Andrés*, and have published a number of short stories, most of them included in the collection *Thank You, Gabe*. Some scenes in all three are drawn from sections of the trilogy. I trust you enjoy reading the novels and short stories as much as I enjoyed writing them.

www.ingramcontent.com/pod-product-compliance
Lightning Source LLC
Chambersburg PA
CBHW070320190726
48291CB00014B/2488